In the Shadow *of the* Enemy

GATLIN FIELDS

Sandra
Waggoner

Sable Creek
PRESS

Cover and text design by Diane King, www.dkingdesigner.com
Maggie photo by Deb Minnard; model Amanda Sheppard
Cover photo of house © 2009 istockphoto.com/Dave Logan
Back cover photo © 2008 dreamstime.com

Scripture taken from the King James Version. Public domain.

Published by Sable Creek Press, PO Box 12217, Glendale, Arizona 85318
www.sablecreekpress.com

Publisher's Cataloging-in-Publication data

Waggoner, Sandra.
    In the shadow of the enemy / Sandra Waggoner.
    p. cm.   "Gatlin Fields"
    Summary: To keep her daddy from going away to find a job, Maggie goes to work for a cruel busybody and learns the truth about God's "heaping coals of kindness."
    ISBN 9780976682363
1. Depressions--1929--Kansas--Juvenile fiction. 2. Family life--Kansas--Fiction. 3. Stepmothers--Juvenile fiction. 4. Fathers and daughters--Juvenile fiction. 5. Christian fiction. I. Title.

PZ7.W124135. In 2009
[Fic]--dc22

                                                            2009923448
Printed in the United States of America.

Chapters

CHAPTER 1

Dust

*T*he door smacked against the church wall, and the vibration surged through the whole building. The congregation rotated from Pastor Olson to look at the man who stood in the back of the church. The man's body shook. He grabbed the hat off his head.

"She's a'comin'!" he belted out. With the passing of his words a dreaded quiet settled in, only to be broken by a low moan. Fingers of wind seeped through the wooden slats, carrying the smell of dust. "I come to warn you! I figure you maybe have twenty minutes afore the worst gets here." With that, the man turned and ran from the church.

"Will there never be an end?" someone whispered.

"How much more can we take?" another mumbled.

"I'm wondering if God even hears us." A depressed voice echoed the thoughts of many in the congregation.

"He hears us!" Pastor Olson broke into the conversation to take charge. "And God loves us. His time is not our time. We need to wait on God, not give up on Him. We all need to keep on asking, because we never know when that last prayer will be the one God answers. With that answer, the rain will come and the dust will go." A gentle smile eased Pastor Olson's reprimand. "Now let's pray, so you can all get to your homes before the storm hits."

Maggie looked at Sue. Her hands were in a tight knot. As soon as the "amen" was said, Sue grabbed the girls and headed for the wagon.

"I wish Daddy was here!" Ruby wailed.

"I'm glad he's not." Sue's voice was as clipped as her steps.

"Why?" Ruby asked.

Opal jabbed her in the side. "Can't you see Mama isn't in a talking mood?"

"Why?" Ruby persisted.

"Because! That's why." Opal glared at Ruby.

"Because? That ain't a why." Ruby stomped her foot.

"Isn't," Opal corrected Ruby's "ain't."

"That's what I just said!" Ruby threw her hands in the air.

Maggie slipped out the door and looked toward the north. A huge wall of black dust was rolling their way. The man had said they had twenty minutes. Twenty minutes? Maybe.

"Opal! Ruby! Stop arguing and get in the wagon!" Maggie yelled, but her words were swept away by a blast of dusty wind. She grabbed the bottom of her dress with one hand and Ruby's arm with the other. "Get in the wagon!" she shouted.

Ruby and Opal tumbled into the wagon bed while Maggie climbed onto the seat beside Sue. Maybe Maggie could help with the horses, since she had known them longer. "You want me to take the reins?" she asked Sue.

Sue was grim. "Can you handle them, Maggie?"

"I think so."

Sue nodded. "If you need help, I'm right here."

Maggie sent a strong wave through the reins and spoke soothingly to the horses. "Come on, Ben. Come on, Maude." Ben and Maude lunged against the harnesses and pulled the wagon into the street.

"Mama?" Maggie peeked at Sue. The word "Mama" still felt strange to use. She didn't understand why, but it made her stomach knot up. Maggie couldn't help glancing at Sue to see if it was really okay with her.

Sue smiled. "Yes, Maggie?"

"Should we take the shortcut?"

Sue paused. Another gust of wind blasted a passing automobile, making it swerve so close to the wagon that the horses reared and jumped toward the boardwalk. The driver blared his horn. People yelled and scrambled for safety. The horses bolted. Sue grabbed the reins while Maggie still held onto them, and together they tried to control the horses.

"Whoa, Ben! Whoa, Maude!" Maggie shouted to the horses, to the wind, to the people as they raced by and to God, if He would please listen.

Finally, she felt the fear ease out of Ben and Maude. Their rampage broke. Lathered, tired and still shaking, the horses slowed and stopped. Maggie let Sue's gentle hands take the reins. Her own hands seemed drawn like a magnet to her heart. The horses had stopped racing, but her heart hadn't.

"Are you okay, Maggie?" Sue asked.

Maggie nodded. She wasn't sure if she was okay or not, but there was no blood to be seen, and her heart was working for sure.

"Why did you do that?" Ruby demanded.

"What?" Maggie turned to gape at Ruby, who was holding onto her sister in a death grip, while Opal had her arms wrapped around the side of the wagon.

Sue stared at Ruby in disbelief. "Ruby!" she warned.

"I don't like the way you drive." Ruby glared at Maggie. "I wish Daddy…"

"Daddy can't be here. He's sick," Opal told her again.

Sue sank back, lowered the reins to her lap and began to laugh.

Ruby squinted. "That wasn't funny."

Maggie stifled a giggle that had bubbled up inside. Ruby didn't like the way she drove? Well, neither did she. Ruby just didn't understand that Maggie hadn't really been driving—she had been trying to stop the horses.

"No, honey, it wasn't funny." Sue handed the reins to Maggie, turned to Ruby and held her arms wide. Ruby plunged into them. "Sometimes it's better to laugh than to cry, and I really didn't want to cry," Sue said. "I wish your daddy had been here, too, but it wouldn't have been good for him. He needs to get better."

"Well, if he had been here, that wouldn't have happened," Ruby persisted. She slid her eyes to Maggie. "He's a gooder driver than you."

"Ruby! That was not Maggie's fault. It was the wind, the auto, the people and even Opal and you screaming. That's what scared the horses," Sue scolded gently. "You tell Maggie 'sorry' right now."

Ruby pulled in a deep breath and pushed out a "sorry" from between clenched teeth.

Maggie nodded, then looked to Sue. "Shortcut?"

Sue gazed ahead. The Gatlin house stood at the top of the hill. They hadn't taken this shortcut since Daddy had come home, and Maggie could tell that Sue didn't want to. Still, the wind whipped at their hair, and a gust of dust belched across the wagon.

"Girls, pull your skirts over your mouths and noses!" Sue ordered. "Maggie, take the shortcut. We need to get home as fast as we can to get out of this storm."

Maggie flipped the reins with a prayer. "Please, Lord, help us!"

The horses pulled the wagon up the hill and through the open gate. Once again, Maggie was in awe at the huge Gatlin house, and at the thought that Sue could have chosen to marry Mr. Thomas Gatlin and live the rest of her life in this mansion without a worry in the world, but instead she had chosen Maggie's very own daddy and her. "Wow!" she yelled into the wind.

"Hold up!" A cracked voice split through the howl of the storm.

Maggie pulled Ben and Maude to a stop. A tall, thin man rolling a whip stepped out of a little house just inside the gate. He came to the side of the wagon and shouted, "This is private property, ladies. You can't pass this way."

"Mr. Johnston, you know who I am. I'm Sue Daniels. Mr. Gatlin has always let me pass through his pasture to get to my home. I live right across there in that boxcar."

Mr. Johnston spat on the ground. "Well, he ain't letting you no more. Them is the orders I got, so you can just turn this here rig around and head home a different way."

"In this storm?" Sue pointed to the wall of dust growing on the horizon. "Surely you could let us cross just this once. We'll not do so again."

"Sorry, but I got my orders and I got my job to think of. Sorry." He put his hand on Maude to start them on their way.

"Hold on there, Martin," a voice broke in from behind him. "You can't mean that!" Valina swayed with her age and her weight, but she made her way from the little house to Mr. Johnston's side.

"Valina, this ain't none of your business. Now, you get on back to the house."

"I will not! Mrs. Sue has been a friend since she was knee-high to a grasshopper. She needs to get home before this storm hits, Martin."

"I got my orders. Mr. Gatlin said it's my job if I let them cross this pasture anymore, and jobs are hard to come by. I'm an old man, Valina. I ain't going to find another job."

Valina raised her hand to the man's face and sweetly traced his lips with her fingertips. Although the wind tore at them, Maggie heard every word Valina spoke. "Martin, we'll get along. Now, I need you to gather the clothes off the line afore this dust hits, and I have to wash Mr. Gatlin's duds again. I'll take care of these ladies for you." Martin hesitated. "Get on with you, now." Valina took the whip from his hand and waved him toward the clothesline at the back of the house.

Martin turned and walked away. Valina shook her head as she watched him. "He's a good man, Mrs. Daniels, he really is, but sometimes he seems to get mixed up as to who is in charge—Mr. Thomas Gatlin or God Almighty!"

"I know he's a good man, Valina." Sue smiled.

"It's just that Mr. Gatlin has been acting out of sorts lately, and Martin is afraid. I keep telling him that with the good Lord's help, we'll make do." Valina shook her head. "Mrs. Daniels, you go on now and cross this here pasture. That storm is a'movin' mighty fast."

"Thank you, Valina. Thank you so much. We'll not forget." Sue turned to Maggie. "Let's get going!"

Maggie shook the reins, and the horses began their journey again. She looked back over her shoulder to see Martin with an armload of clothes and Valina at his side. Maggie hoped he wouldn't lose his job. Mr. Johnston was okay, but Valina had just found a special place in Maggie's heart.

When they reached the gate between the two pastures, Sue jumped down and swung it open. Maggie spurred the horses through, then paused and waited for Sue to climb aboard. "We've got to hurry!" Sue shouted. "It's coming fast!"

They had gone barely ten more yards when the storm hit. Dust swirled and pelted Maggie's cheeks. She squinted until she hardly had her eyes open.

"Maggie, stop at the front of the house and let the girls out," Sue yelled over the wind. "You can help me with the horses."

Maggie pulled the team up before the old boxcar. Ruby and Opal jumped out and ran up the front steps. With one hand, Maggie grabbed her skirt and held it over her face to keep the thick dust out. Ben and Maude pawed the ground, tugging and trying to reach the shelter of the shed. "I can take the team to the shed so you can check on Daddy," Maggie told Sue.

Sue paused only for a glance, then nodded. "I'll check on your daddy and get the wet towels for the windows. Be careful!" She jumped to the ground and ran for the house.

Maggie let Ben and Maude have their heads. They almost ran to the shed. Maggie unhitched the two, led them to the inside corner farthest away from the billowing dust, and tied them so they wouldn't go crazy during the storm and leave the shed. She threw them a couple of armloads of hay and promised something better after the storm.

Then she turned and looked toward the house. Nothing. The sky was blacker than midnight, with no stars. The wind roared. She had to keep her nose and mouth covered so she could breathe. Can I make it to the house? she wondered. She knew the way, but she couldn't see, and she would have to fight the wind. The howling of the wind mixed up the other, more familiar sounds. She might lose her way. She looked back into the barn and watched the dust swirling up from the dirt floor. The boxcar would be better than this. She plunged into the storm.

A blast of wind whipped through the dust, yanked her clothes and tore at her hair. Maggie lost her balance, stumbled and fell. The wind howled and moaned. Maggie could feel the dust in her ears, between her fingers and beneath her clothes. She clamped her eyes shut. The world as she had always known it existed no more. There was only the dark, howling dust monster that sifted through any minute crevice it could find. She couldn't stay here. The dust would eat at her and scour her away to nothing.

She struggled to her feet. Maybe if I shout loud enough, someone from the house will yell back. Then I might be able to follow the sound. Maggie shouted the closest thing to her heart. "Daddy! Help! God in my heart, help! Daddy! Daddy, help! God in my heart, help!"

She listened. Only the roar of the dust storm returned her cries.

She pushed to her feet, ran, stumbled and fell again. Crawling, she felt along the ground and found the fence. If she could follow the fence to the gate, she would be right in front of the house.

The wind fought Maggie. She couldn't stand, so she continued to crawl as she held onto the fence. Her heart pounded. Yes! She found the gate. Again she began to shout. Her mouth filled with dirt. Her nose—she couldn't breathe! Maggie choked and coughed until she thought she would die. She lay flat on the ground, covering her head with her arms. When she finally caught her breath, she fell silent.

"Maggie!" Faintly, she heard her name called over and over again. The voice sounded like Mama's. Had Maggie died? She opened her eyes. No, she hadn't died. She was still in the middle of the dust storm, and she knew there wouldn't be any of those in heaven.

"Maggie!" Again the familiar voice called. Sue. It was Sue, her new mama. Maggie pulled her body up and dragged herself on hands and knees toward the sound. She felt the worn path to the steps, and like a well-practiced reader of Braille she quickened her pace. The voice was closer.

"Sue!" Maggie gagged the word out. She heard the screen door fly open and slap wildly against the side of the porch. She was almost at the house. Her hand reached out and grabbed the bottom step.

"Maggie!" Swift, strong arms reached down and pulled her up the rest of the steps to the porch and into the house. "Maggie, honey, are you all right?" Sue sat on the floor and rocked her. "Opal! Ruby! Bring some wet cloths!" Gently, she sponged Maggie's face, then handed her a glass of water. "Maggie, swish your mouth out before you swallow."

Maggie asked no questions. She just did as she was told. The dust in her mouth tasted like the rain they needed so badly. When she could talk, she looked up at Sue. "I thought you were my mama when I heard you calling my name." She swallowed. "I thought I had died and gone to heaven, but then I opened my eyes."

Sue whispered, "Maggie, I'm so sorry I'm not your real mama, but I'll try to be the best I can. I'm very glad that you didn't die."

Ruby's eyes flashed with horror. "You mean Maggie could have died out there in that old dust storm?"

Sue nodded.

Opal dropped beside Maggie. "Maggie, don't you ever die!"

"Never!" Ruby lassoed Maggie's neck with her arms and held tight.

"Well, don't strangle her now!" Opal warned.

Maggie giggled. It was good to have sisters.

Sue interrupted gently. "Maggie, was your daddy in the shed?"

Maggie's heart skipped a beat and pounded in her ears. "Daddy's not in here?"

Sue shook her head.

Maggie gulped. "Daddy wasn't in the shed. At least, I didn't see him before the dust storm hit." She paused, then whispered, "Lulubelle wasn't in the shed, either."

Sue closed her eyes.

Opal was the one who spoke all their thoughts aloud. "Do you think Daddy went after Lulubelle?"

Maggie met Opal's gaze. "Yes. That is exactly what he would do."

"We got to go get him," Ruby wailed.

"No! No one goes out in this storm. We almost lost Maggie, and I'll not chance anyone. Not anyone! Is that understood?"

"But what will we do?" Opal asked.

"We will pray," Sue whispered.

After the Storm

*E*ven though the windows were closed, the wet towels that hung over them billowed like heavy-breathing swamp monsters caked with mud. Sue had tucked a rolled rag rug beneath the door, but a scum of grit covered the floor. Dust settled on every piece of furniture in the house. For hours, the wind howled and moaned. With the dust came a hopelessness that sapped all energy from the body and from the soul as well.

Ruby had fallen asleep in a blanketed heap on the floor because she refused to go to the bedroom. There was no way she was going to be separated from the rest of them. It made Maggie hot to see Ruby all covered up. At least the blanket would keep the dust off her—maybe.

Opal tried to look through an old newspaper, but she ended up drawing stick figures in the dust on the floor. Maggie watched her draw with her finger and then erase her sketches by blowing, as if she were blowing out candles on a cake.

Sue sat in the rocker holding her Bible. She had read it and

read it some more. Then she leaned back, rocking slowly and staring at nothing Maggie could see. Streaks of tears left a path down the light film of dust on her face.

Maggie wished she knew how to help Sue, but she was drained of all ideas. If only she could stop the storm! She knew the God in her heart could, but if he hadn't done it for Sue, why would he do it for Maggie? Sue had known him a lot longer and a lot better. What was it Pastor Olson had said? It was something about not giving up on God … that maybe your prayer would be the next one He would answer. Maggie wondered just how pastors knew all this stuff. Maybe she should try and ask God again to stop the raging dust storm.

She dropped her head in her hands and felt the grit grind against her cheeks. "God," she whispered, "please stop this horrible storm. My daddy's out there." She pulled her head up to listen. The windy howls swept about their boxcar home. Maggie lifted her eyes to the ceiling. "Please!" she begged.

She rested her head against the wall and closed her eyes. Maybe she could sleep. Her thoughts danced back in time. She was lying on the ground beneath cottonwood branches that filtered the sun's warm rays.

"Hey!" Opal stopped drawing. "Hey, do you hear that?"

"What?" Maggie flipped her eyes open.

"Nothing!" Opal giggled.

"What? What did you want me to hear?"

"Nothing. Nothing at all!" Opal jumped up and spread her arms wide.

Sue stopped rocking. "Opal's right. There's nothing to hear."

Maggie jumped to her feet. "The storm is over?"

Sue nodded. "Thank God!"

"Yes! He did it!" Maggie grabbed Opal and they danced in circles, their feet gliding and sliding through the dust. They laughed and fell in a clumsy heap on top of Ruby.

"Hey, you big lugs, get off me!" Ruby pushed the girls.

Maggie and Opal yanked Ruby into their celebration. "The storm is over! The storm is over!" they chanted.

Maggie looked at Sue. She was smoothing her dress down. "I'm going to look for your daddy. We only have a few hours until it gets dark."

"Can I come, too?" Maggie asked. She saw the hesitation in Sue's eyes and tagged on a "please!"

"Okay. Ruby, you get a broom. Opal, you get a bucket of water and start cleaning." Sue turned toward the door.

"But…" the girls protested.

"No buts! Someone needs to be here if your daddy gets here before we find him. Maggie, let's go."

Sue and Maggie stepped out the door, walked across the porch and opened the screen door. The outside was so bright that Maggie had to shade her eyes. After the continual howling of the wind, the quiet was suffocating. Maggie felt as if a shroud of silence and dust had been dropped over her.

Sue lowered her voice. "Maggie, honey, you know your daddy wasn't feeling very well. We may need the wagon to get him home when we find him."

Maggie blinked. She knew Sue was trying to tell her something, and it must be something serious. Maggie searched her new mama's face. "Daddy's all right. He is strong. I've seen him carry feed sacks and hay bales and move the plow, and he can even carry me. He carried you through the door when you got married. Daddy's all right. He's got to be!" Maggie was on the verge of panic.

"Maggie." Sue wrapped her arms around her. For a long moment they stood, hugged and hoped together. Finally, Sue broke the silence. "I think the pasture would be the place to start. If we need the wagon, we'll come back and get it." She held Maggie's hand.

They rounded the corner of the boxcar and scanned the pasture. As they watched, a figure that looked like a big boulder, or maybe a rock, lunged to its feet and shook. A dust cloud rose, swirled and settled. It wasn't a boulder at all. It was Lulubelle.

Maggie dropped Sue's hand and ran. Where Lulubelle was, Daddy was sure to be. "Lulubelle! Daddy!" she called. She skidded to a stop beside Lulubelle and swung in a circle. "Lulubelle, where is Daddy?"

Sue ran up beside her. "Maggie?"

"I don't know. I thought that Daddy would be right with Lulubelle, but he's not." Maggie reached out and put her hand against the old cow. A dust puff exploded and settled. "Now what will we do?"

Sue scanned the pasture.

"I know!" Maggie ran to the big cottonwood. "I can see all around from up here." She latched onto the bottom branch and swung up into the tree. This was her world. She loved trees, and cottonwoods were her favorite. There were five cottonwoods on the farm, and she knew each one by heart. The branches were huge. She could lie on them and watch the sun dapple her skin, while the leaves danced and clinked against each other like muffled wind chimes.

"Be careful, Maggie," Sue warned. Maggie wound her way up the tree. "Do you see him?"

"No."

"Are you sure?"

"Nothing!"

Sue licked her lips. "Maggie, look carefully. He might be lying down on the ground."

"Why?"

"Honey, I…" Sue stumbled into silence.

"Mama! Maggie!" Opal came running around the house, yelling. "Come quick!"

Sue turned from the tree. Maggie froze. She couldn't see anything, but they must have found Daddy. She watched as Sue took three steps in slow motion toward the house and then built to a run. Maggie dropped from branch to branch until she was close enough to jump to the ground, then she ran, too.

Together, Sue and Maggie came to a stop in front of Opal. Daddy wasn't there.

"Opal?" Sue asked.

Opal's eyes were big. She pointed to the front of the house. An old, well-kept wagon was hitched to the fence. Maggie heard the screen door screech as Valina pushed it open.

"Mrs. Sue? I got your man inside here." Valina spread her face in a smile that made Maggie feel warm.

"Valina? What's going on?" Sue asked.

"Now, Mrs. Sue, you'd best come on in and see for your own self." Valina eased away from the door and let them in. "I had that little Opal of yours boil some water for tea." Valina followed them into the house.

Daddy was in the rocker. For sure, he needed a bath. There was so much dust on him that Maggie couldn't tell what color his clothes were. He looked like a raccoon—the only clean patches on his face were around his eyes. He breathed heavily, coughing.

Maggie dropped beside his chair, Ruby and Opal crowding behind. "Daddy, we were looking for you. Where have you been?"

Daddy could only cough. Sue came to his rescue. "Maggie, Daddy will tell us all about it later. First we need to clean him up, and he most likely needs to go to bed."

"Most likely he needs a doctor." Valina pulled a chair from the table. "Mrs. Sue, you just sit yourself beside your man, and I'll bring you some warm water and a cloth. Then you can get him cleaned up."

"Thank you, Valina." Sue took the chair.

"Mrs. Sue, do you want me to fetch Dr. Nelson?" Valina asked.

"Valina, I can't," Sue whispered.

"Missy, your man needs a doctor." Valina looked deep into her eyes.

"Valina, I can't," Sue repeated. "We have no money."

"Mama, what about the money Daddy brought home from the salt mines? We could use it." Maggie took Sue's hand.

"We did use it. We paid the bank note on the farm, honey."

"All of it?" Maggie asked.

"It's gone. All gone."

Valina leaned in close to Sue. "Mrs. Sue, you know Dr. Nelson would give credit to you."

Sue shook her head. "Sam would never let me do that. We agreed about credit before we were married."

Valina pushed her lips together and nodded her head. "Trust is important," she sighed. "We'll just put our heads together and do the best we can. I got some herbs back at the house what might help. Maybe your girl here could come with me to fetch them when I go."

"I'll go." Maggie smiled.

"Me, too!" Ruby flashed a pleading look at Valina.

"Don't leave me out," Opal joined in.

Valina rumbled with a deep, musical laugh. "I'd be glad to take you all, but I ain't going just yet. Your mama and I got some more talking to do."

"Valina, do the girls need to leave us for a bit?" Sue spoke quietly.

"No. I reckon they had best hear this from a friend. It'll be sounding better." Valina swayed to the table and pulled out a chair. "Now, Mrs. Sue, afore I sit, if you are done cleaning your man I'll help you get him to bed. He'll rest better there."

"Thanks, Valina." Between Sue and Valina, Daddy struggled to get out of the rocker. He smiled, but a coughing fit surged through him when he tried to talk. He gave up on what he was trying to say and let them help him to the bedroom. Maggie heard the bed creak. Then Valina stepped back out of the room.

Maggie couldn't help it. Silent tears slid down her face. Never had she seen Daddy like this.

Valina settled in her chair close to Maggie and scooped Maggie's head into her lap. With one hand she patted her, while with the other she combed Maggie's hair with her fingers. "Little Missy, the good Lord is going to help your daddy. You just believe in that."

Sue pulled the bedroom door closed behind her and slipped over to the rocker. She took a deep breath. "Now, Valina, what is this we need to hear from a friend?"

"Well, let me tell you, Mrs. Sue. In the dark part of the storm, Martin jumped out of his chair. It seemed he done forgot he had staked Daisy behind the barn, and, being she is going to have a calf any day now, Martin thought he needed to go get her. So he wrapped a wet kerchief around his face, grabbed a lantern and took off out the door." Valina absently ran her fingers through Maggie's hair. "Whilst Martin was gone, Mr. Gatlin come pounding on my door. He wanted Martin, but I told him he was out with Daisy, so he left." Valina sighed heavily and shook her head.

Maggie raised her head and waited with wide eyes for Valina to finish her story.

"Later, Martin came back carrying your man. He had just set him at the kitchen table when Mr. Gatlin come a'poundin' on our door again. This time, Martin answered the door, because I was seeing to your man. I heard Mr. Gatlin a'yellin' about seeing a trespasser out by the barn. He was saying that as soon as his telephone started working again he was going to call the sheriff and press charges, and if the blamed telephone didn't start working after the storm he was going to send Martin to get the sheriff. Then your man started coughing, and Mr. Gatlin asked who was that, so I come to the kitchen door and whooped up a coughing storm so Mr. Gatlin would think it was me."

Valina demonstrated her coughing fit, which made Ruby giggle. Opal jabbed her in the ribs. Valina chuckled and began again. "Martin told him I get that way with every one of those woe-begotten dust storms. Then Martin up and says, 'Mr. Gatlin, as soon as this storm settles a bit more, I was going to take Valina to Dr. Nelson. Would that be fine?' Mr. Gatlin

looked at me a long time, so I coughed some more. Finally, he said it would be fine. Then he told Martin to stop by the sheriff's and send him out. After Mr. Gatlin left, Martin hitched the team and pulled the wagon to the back of the house. We hid your man in the back of the wagon and threw a quilt over him. I hated to do that to him, but I didn't want Mr. Gatlin to find him. Anyway, Martin left the rig for us while he went to get the sheriff."

"Sheriff?" Maggie could keep silent no longer. "Does that mean Daddy will be arrested and go to jail?"

"Now, now, Missy. Don't you be a'worryin'. Mr. Thomas Gatlin only thinks he's God." Valina chuckled.

Maggie wasn't sure she understood what Valina had just said, but it made her feel better. "Valina, does Mr. Gatlin know that the trespasser was Sam?" Sue asked.

Valina dropped her eyes. "No. He don't know it was your man, but that's what he wants to think. He's got something eating at his craw, and I am thinking it's because you didn't marry him."

"Valina!" Sue drummed her fingers on the arm of the rocker and shook her head. "I hope not."

"Well, if it is, he'd best get over it." Valina gave a final nod.

"Valina, will Martin tell Mr. Gatlin or the sheriff?"

Valina chuckled. "Not if he knows what's good for him."

"Really?" Sue smiled. "What about his job? I know he was worried about it."

"Well now, the way I have it figured, my Martin will keep his lips sealed, because what Mr. Gatlin don't know won't hurt him and it could hurt us. Besides Martin, the only ones who know who that trespasser was are right here in this room."

Slowly, her eyes passed to each of the girls.

"Girls, this news does not go outside these walls. Is that understood?" Sue warned.

"Yes, ma'am," Ruby was the first to promise.

Opal held her right hand up. "I'll swear on the Bible, cross my heart and hope to die."

"You better be sure you don't blab!" Ruby jabbed Opal.

Maggie merely nodded.

"With all these promises, I think our secret is safe." Valina winked at Sue. "And we had best be on our way if we're going to get those doctoring things back afore midnight." She heaved herself out of the chair.

"Valina, are you sure you and Martin will be all right?" Sue asked again.

"Mrs. Sue, it's in bigger hands than Mr. Thomas Gatlin's." Valina stretched her arms wide, inviting the girls. "Are you ladies coming with me?"

Ruby and Opal were the first to latch onto her hands. Maggie looked to Sue.

"It's fine, Maggie. Go on. Your daddy and I will be here, and I won't let anything happen to him."

Maggie swallowed. "If Daddy wakes up, will you tell him I love him?"

"It will be the very first thing I tell him, Maggie." Sue bent to brush the top of her head with a kiss. "Now, off with you!"

Valina held the door for the three little girls. She smiled at Sue. "Don't you worry, Mrs. Sue." As she turned to leave, she crooned, "I don't know what comes on the morrow, but I know who holds my hand!"

CHAPTER 3

Arrested

"Valina's a funny name." Ruby's elbows rested on the seat of the buckboard with her hands cradling her chin.

"Shush, you dunce! That isn't something you say to people," Opal scolded.

"I'm not a dunce. And that for sure is something you're not to say to people." Ruby stuck her tongue out.

"Your face will get stuck that way."

"It will not."

"Will, too!"

"Ruby, Opal, quit!" Maggie called from the back of the wagon.

Valina's rich chuckle brought silence to the three. "The little one is right. Valina is a funny name, but there isn't one single soul walking this earth aside of me with that name. My mama gave me a mouthful of name the day I was born, but nobody ever called me by it since."

"What is the mouthful of name?" Ruby asked what they all wanted to know.

"Valina Maeleen Manuella Steele."

"Wow!" Opal whistled. "That is a mouthful, all right."

"Now who's the dunce?" Ruby chided.

"Girls!" Maggie warned.

"It be all right, Missy. It don't bother me. Fact is, I always hoped to have three little girls and call each by one of those names. Spread out a bit, they be good names. It's just when you put them all together it becomes quite a mouthful."

"How come you didn't have three little girls?" Ruby wanted to know.

Opal jabbed her. "You're just Miss Busybody, aren't you?"

"I am not. I am making polite conversation."

"That is not polite."

"And just why isn't it?"

"Because it's nosey."

"You two will make Mrs. Valina glad she didn't have those three girls." Maggie stopped the argument.

"The truth be known, I did have those three girls." Valina gazed into the distance.

"Oh, they would be great friends. Can they come and play?" Ruby wanted to know.

"Ruby!" Opal shook her head in wonder. "They would be Mama's age."

"They would?"

"Yes, Ruby, they would," Maggie confirmed. Then she turned to Opal to remind her, "Remember, Ruby is only five."

"Valina, do little Valina and Maeleen and … and … I forgot the other one … do they have girls?" Ruby asked.

"Manuella. No, child. They never had a chance to have any children. Martin and I buried all three of them on the same sad day. It was the influenza that took them. A part of me died with them, it just didn't get covered in the grave. Martin hasn't ever been the same. Oh, he's still a right loving man. I guess it's his laughter I miss." Valina heaved a sigh as she pulled the wagon to a stop behind her house. "I'll be right back. You stay here."

Silence settled over the wagon. Ruby, Opal and Maggie didn't know what to say to Valina. Maggie wished there was a way she could make her feel better, but she didn't know how. She looked up into the evening sky. Stars were just beginning to twinkle. She squinted to search out heaven. "God, why did that happen to Mrs. Valina and Mr. Martin? Please make them feel better."

Valina opened the door. She had scooped the corners of her apron into a pocket that bulged with doctoring stuff.

"Valina, you can't go!" Martin's voice was a whisper, but it was harsh enough that Maggie heard it.

"I can't not go, Martin." Valina's voice was low but firm. "It's the only chance Mrs. Sue's man has got."

Martin had followed Valina out the door and across the porch. "I'm telling you, Mr. Gatlin left with the sheriff, and they were headed for Mrs. Sue's place. If Mr. Gatlin finds you there, he's going to know we helped Mrs. Sue's man. Then we won't have a job. We won't have a house to live in. We won't have nothing!"

"Then, Martin, we'll have nothing. We done it afore. We can do it again."

"Stop and think, Valina." Martin turned her to face him. "You know what else it will mean if they find you over there?"

Valina shook her head.

"It will mean that Mr. Sam was the trespasser. You knowing

about Mrs. Sue's man would be the only way Mr. Gatlin and the sheriff could place him on Mr. Gatlin's property."

Valina moaned.

"Mr. Gatlin is dead set on having Mr. Sam arrested and thrown in jail. If you go waltzing in there knowing he needs doctoring, you'll give it away."

Valina stood and toyed with the ends of her gathered apron. She sighed. "What to do? What to do? Without doctoring, he won't make it. With doctoring, it be chancy. If they throw him in jail…" She let it hang.

Maggie knew what Valina meant. She meant that Daddy might die. He couldn't! God wouldn't do that. But God had let Mama die. God had let Opal and Ruby's daddy die. God had let all three of Valina's girls die. Maggie wanted to scream. If God loved us so much, just why did he let people die? She jerked her thoughts back. The one thing she knew for sure was that Valina had said that if Daddy didn't get the medicine, he would die.

Maggie flung herself out of the wagon and ran to Valina. "Let us take the medicine to Daddy! Then they won't know where it came from."

"Alone? Child, it be 'most dark!"

"All three of us can go. We won't be afraid if we're together," Maggie begged.

"I'm scared!" Ruby's eyes were huge.

"Ruby, I'll be on one side of you and Opal can be on the other. We won't let anything happen to you. Promise! Right, Opal?"

All eyes turned to Opal. Her face was as pale as the moon that was rising in the darkening night. Slowly, she nodded her head. No words would come out.

Valina shook her head. "It won't work, Martin. It won't work. They're just babies. They're too little and too scared."

Martin laid out a plan. "It'll work, Valina. I'll take them. We'll cut across the pasture, and I'll take them close enough that they can see the door. I'll watch until they get in the house. Then I'll just sneak away."

Valina was hesitant.

"It will work, Valina." Martin stroked her shoulder.

"We won't be afraid if Mr. Johnston comes with us," Maggie said, looking at Opal and Ruby in the hope that they would confirm what she said.

Opal was still. Ruby slipped out of the wagon to stand beside Mr. Johnston. "Will you hold my hand?"

The hard, solid wall Mr. Johnston had built around himself began to crumble. A quiet "yes" was all he muttered.

"Well, I want his other hand." Opal jumped down and ran to his side.

Valina's eyes glittered in the moonlight. "Miracles!" she whispered.

Maggie was ready to go. "I'll carry the medicine."

Valina untied the apron from around her waist and cinched the bundle tight, so that it would be easy for Maggie to carry. "God his own self be with you!"

Maggie was glad the moon shone light on their way, but it was eerie, too. The shadows cast by the dancing light could easily become wild animals or monsters. She almost wished Mr. Johnston had three hands, so she could hold one, too.

The air was so dry that not many mosquitoes buzzed. Once, a grasshopper slammed into her forehead, and she stifled a scream. The dry pasture grass crunched and belched dust with each step. That made her think about rattlesnakes. She knew they lived in the pasture, because Sue had warned her about them.

Ruby must have read her thoughts. "Mr. Johnston, what about rattlers?"

"Don't you worry none. It's nighttime. I imagine they scuttled up in some hole." He tried to reassure her.

"But I think I heard one," she whined.

"Must have been a locust. Sometimes they sound like rattlers," Mr. Johnston explained.

"Nope!" Ruby shook her head.

Mr. Johnston swung Ruby to his shoulders, and there she stayed for the rest of the journey. "Quiet, now," he warned. "We're getting close to the house."

To Maggie's ears, the sound of her own breathing was as loud as a roaring waterfall. She tried to hold it, but it spilled out of her body on a rampage. Slowly, they slipped from the back of the house around to the front.

Maggie froze. The blue Hudson that belonged to Mr. Gatlin sat on the road beside the sheriff's car. She could hear voices. They sounded as though they were arguing, but she couldn't understand what they said.

Mr. Johnston easily set Ruby on the ground. For a moment, he stood still. "If you ladies give me to the count of twenty before you head to the house, it will give me time to get to that tree yonder and hunker down so I can watch you safe to the door. I'd be much obliged."

Maggie nodded and began to count. Twenty seemed as far away as two thousand. She shifted Valina's apron in her hand. The hot bodies of Opal and Ruby were squished against her.

"Is it twenty yet?" Ruby whispered.

"I don't know," Maggie breathed.

"You're supposed to be counting!" Opal hissed.

Maggie looked behind her and searched the darkness. She couldn't see even a shadow that might be Mr. Johnston. He must be behind the tree. She waved in the darkness. "Okay, let's go in."

The steps creaked. Opal let the screen door slam and the front door groan. None of these noises stopped the argument that was going on inside.

"I own you, Sheriff. I am the one who got you elected, and I am the one who can remove you from office," Mr. Gatlin bellowed.

"No one owns me, Thomas. I don't care what you did that might have helped me into office. You do not own me. I took an oath to uphold the law, not to uphold you." The sheriff's nose was only inches away from Mr. Gatlin's.

"If you do not have that man arrested tonight, I will go to a higher authority first thing in the morning and have you removed from office." Mr. Gatlin's face was purple.

"Thomas, be sensible! That man cannot be your trespasser. You saw him. I don't even think he can get out of bed." The sheriff held out his hands.

Sue was pale, but she stood firmly blocking the bedroom door. "Gentlemen, please! The girls are home."

The sheriff turned. "Sorry, ma'am."

"The shouting can't be good for my husband, and I would rather the girls not hear it." Sue was every bit a lady.

Thomas Gatlin glared at her.

"Sorry, ma'am," the sheriff apologized again.

"Are you going to do your duty and arrest this man?" Mr. Gatlin slammed his fist into his hand.

The sheriff sighed. "I am going to do my duty, Thomas."

Sue's hand flew to her throat. "No," she mouthed.

Maggie ran to Sue's side to help her bar the door. "No! You cannot take my daddy to jail. He will die. I won't let you!" Sobbing, she sank to the floor. "I can't live without my daddy. I can't! I just can't!"

Opal and Ruby stomped over to stand in front of Maggie and the door. "We just got our new daddy. We won't let you have him." Opal crossed her arms.

"Go away!" Ruby crossed her arms, just like Opal.

"Good. I'm glad you came to your senses, Sheriff. Duty is an important thing, and I'm glad you are going to do it." Mr. Gatlin beamed with victory. "I'll help you any way I can. Why, I'll even help you carry him out to the car."

"That won't be necessary, Thomas." The sheriff paused. With a gleam in his eye, he added, "My duty, Mr. Gatlin, is to ask you to leave. You are disturbing the peace of this home."

"What?"

"You need to leave, Mr. Gatlin."

"Are you out of your mind?" Mr. Gatlin turned a deeper shade of purple. "I'll have your job for this!"

The sheriff pulled his handcuffs off his belt and dangled them in front of Mr. Gatlin. "Are you going to leave, or do I arrest you?"

Mr. Gatlin could only sputter. He looked from the sheriff to Sue. Then he turned and tromped out the door. He marched to his car, yanked the door open and slammed it closed. The Hudson's wheels spun in the dirt, then caught. The car rolled out of the yard and down the road.

In the quiet that settled, Sue looked at the sheriff. "Can he have your job?"

The sheriff shrugged. "Legally? No. Mr. Thomas Gatlin owns a lot of Ford County and a lot of its people, but he doesn't own me."

"Thank you, Sheriff."

"I'm just sorry it happened, ma'am." He tipped his hat. "I'll be leaving now. Good luck with your husband. Maybe you can all get some rest." The sheriff turned and left.

Sue sank to the floor beside Maggie. "Maggie, that was close! I was never so glad to see you girls in all my life."

CHAPTER 4

No Credit

Four days drudged by as Maggie's daddy lay unawake and feverish. Sue had moved the rocker to Daddy's bedside, where she and Maggie took turns keeping vigil. There were changes in Daddy, but they weren't good. His cheeks were hollow, and dark stubble sprouted over his face. Maggie couldn't help but think how happy everyone would be if their wheat crop had sprouted so well.

Daddy hadn't even planted wheat last fall, because the ground was too dry. He had kept waiting for rain, but it still hadn't come. Everything was crispy, stifling, dry. Daddy said it was a wonder the trees had even budded this spring. Maybe their roots went deep enough to find what little water must be under the ground, somewhere. No rain. That was why Daddy had had to get another job—so he could save the farm.

Just how it worked that he'd married Sue was something Maggie wasn't sure about. He had told her she needed a mama, because he didn't know how to teach her to be a young lady. Maggie thought he had done a good job so far. As she thought of all this, a thin smile warmed her. Sue was nice to have.

Maggie leaned her head back in the rocker, closed her eyes and whispered her whole name. Margaret Pearl Daniels. Sue had wanted Maggie to have a precious-jewel name like her other two girls, so she had let her pick out whatever jewel name she wanted. Maggie had chosen Pearl, because pearls were so creamy and reflected pastel rainbows. Then Sue had asked Maggie to give her a precious name in return: Mama.

Maggie turned it over in her heart. She hadn't called anyone by that name since her own mama had died. Would it make Maggie a traitor to her mama? Would it hurt Mama's feelings? Could Mama hear Maggie up in heaven?

If there was anyone in the whole wide world Maggie wanted to call Mama, it was Sue. Sue had told her how to have the God of heaven live in her heart. Maggie thought Sue loved her, and it made her feel warm inside. Yet the couple of times she had called her Mama, it had made her stomach roll.

Maggie shoved the thought aside. She would rather think about her own wonderful name. "What a miracle! Margaret Pearl Daniels. Wow! A precious jewel." Maggie giggled.

"That sounds like my Maggie." A hoarse voice broke into her thoughts.

"Daddy!" Maggie shouted. "Daddy! You're alive!"

Daddy gave a chuckle-cough. "Well, if I'm dead, you must be an angel." He tried to laugh, but coughing racked his body.

"Be still!" Maggie ordered. "I'll get Sue." She flew to the bedroom door and hollered, "Hey, everyone! Daddy's awake!"

Sue was the first one in the room. Opal and Ruby tumbled over each other to pile in behind her. Sue sat on the edge of the bed and felt Daddy's forehead for the fever that had raged through his body these last few days. Maggie could tell by Sue's furrowed brow that the fever must still be there.

Ruby dove on the bed. "Daddy!" She grabbed his head with her chubby hands and splashed kisses on his cheeks. "Ooh! You feel all stickery!" Ruby giggled.

Maggie felt a familiar pang of jealousy. She liked having Opal and Ruby for sisters, but sharing her daddy was hard to do. She wondered how come they didn't have trouble calling her daddy "Daddy," when it was hard for her to call Sue Mama.

Daddy laughed and ended up coughing again.

"Ruby, get off the bed. See, you hurt Daddy," Opal scolded.

Maggie had wanted to say the same thing. She was glad Opal said it.

"I did not!"

"You made him start coughing."

"I did not!"

"Girls," Sue spoke quietly, "I'm just as sure that he doesn't need your arguing. Ruby, off the bed."

"Told you so!" Opal had to have the last word. Grandly, Ruby rolled out her tongue.

"Girls!"

Maggie laughed. Opal and Ruby seemed to be at odds all the time, but somehow it made them happy.

"Girls, why don't each of you tell your daddy a quick hi and bye, so he can get rested from your visit," Sue suggested.

Opal's eyebrows rose. "But we just got here."

"Yes, you did. Now you are going to leave." Sue stood and pulled Ruby off the bed.

"Why do we have to go?" Ruby wanted to know.

"Because I said so, and because I am your mother, and because if you don't, you will be in trouble." Sue pointed to the door.

Maggie dropped her gaze to the floor. She wondered why she had to go, too. Sure, Ruby and Opal were making noise, but she wasn't.

Sue stopped her. "Maggie, you may come and give your daddy a hug before you go."

Maggie looked at Sue. She seemed always to know what was going on inside Maggie, even when Maggie herself wasn't sure what was happening.

"Thank you." She stepped over to the bed and gave her daddy a gentle hug, then tiptoed out of the room after the other two.

Ruby's bottom lip hung. "I still don't know why we had to leave."

Opal wasted no time in telling her. "Because you jumped on Daddy. That's why!"

"I jumped on the bed, not on Daddy."

"Well, you missed."

"Did not!"

"Did too!"

After Maggie had slipped out of the bedroom, she quietly slid down the wall to the floor and sat there. Daddy was better, she could tell. It still scared her, though, to see him like this. How long would he be this way? She closed her eyes and leaned her head against the wall.

"Sam, Dr. Nelson would let me have credit. I've known him all my life."

Maggie's eyes flew open. She could hear them word for word through the cardboarded door of the bedroom.

"No credit, Sue! We agreed on that before we married." Daddy's voice was low and slow.

"Sam, Valina and I have done all we can to make you better, and I'm afraid. I'm afraid it's not enough. Please, Sam," Sue begged.

Maggie knew she should leave. She remembered how much trouble she had gotten into before for eavesdropping, but she felt like she was in a trance. She had to know the answer to Sue's question.

A volcano of coughing surged through the house. Ruby and Opal stopped their bickering and looked at the bedroom door, with Maggie beside it. Quickly, Maggie put her finger to her lips, telling them to not say a word. Ruby opened her mouth to speak. Opal smashed her hand on top of Ruby's lips and kept it there. "Hush!" she ordered.

"I don't like credit, Sue. It's a road that only goes downhill, and it's hard to get back up—if you ever do."

"I don't like it, either, but I don't want to lose you, Sam. If you die, what good will it do me that I don't owe anyone? Sam, please!" Sue sounded desperate.

"Sell Lulubelle."

"I've been selling her milk. Right now, that is our only source of income."

Ruby broke away from Opal. Tears flooded her eyes. "Is Daddy going to die?"

"I don't know," Opal whispered.

Both girls looked to Maggie. Maggie bit her lip. Now she wished she hadn't heard a word from behind the closed door. She stood, walked softly to the front door of the house and put her hand on the knob. She needed to be alone. When she got out the door, she was going to run. She didn't know where. Anywhere would do, as long as she was alone and away from here. What would happen to her if Daddy died?

"Maggie, where are you going?" Opal asked.

Maggie looked back, choked down her sobs and yelled, "I don't know!" She turned and ran.

She ran across the porch, out the door, down the steps and smack dab into a man she had never seen before. She tumbled, and his black bag went flying.

"Whoa now, little lady!" He reached down and pulled her to her feet.

Maggie sucked in her breath. Her eyes traveled up to one of the kindest faces she had ever seen. She didn't even try to say anything. She just stared. By this time, Opal and Ruby had plunged out of the house in pursuit of Maggie.

"Hey, Maggie! You found Dr. Nelson." Opal voice was filled with awe.

"So that's where you were going," Ruby added.

"Maggie, is it?" Dr. Nelson had a deep, scratchy voice.

Maggie nodded.

"Valina came by to see me. She happened to mention that your daddy was a little under the weather."

"Mama thinks he's going to die," Ruby blurted out.

"Can you fix him?" Opal wanted to know.

Dr. Nelson cleared his throat. "I'll tell you what I can do. I can look at him and try my very best. After all, these little ladies need their daddy."

"Come quick!" Ruby motioned for him to follow her. Opal grabbed his hand and tugged.

Dr. Nelson chuckled. "Youth! It never ceases to amaze me.

Hold your horses, ladies. I need my bag."

Maggie picked it up and handed it to him. With a pleading look, she whispered, "Please save him!"

As they walked into the boxcar house, Sue came out of the bedroom. "Dr. Nelson! What are you doing here?"

Maggie watched as the kind face smiled. Peace swept over her, and she knew. She knew that it was probably Valina who had told him, but it was God in heaven who had sent him.

"Sue, Valina stopped by my office. She didn't ask me to come. She just asked me what else she could do for your man. I told her I couldn't know that without looking at him."

"Dr. Nelson, we can't pay you, and Sam won't let us ask for credit. He told me to sell the cow. That means we'll have to wait until we can sell Lulubelle," Sue explained.

"Wait just a minute. Now, I already told you I'm here because Valina wanted to know what else she could do. That means I'm helping Valina with her medical education. I don't charge for such as that. This town can use another medically educated person. So I guess you could say you are helping Dodge City, Kansas. Now, will you let me see Valina's patient?"

"Valina's patient?" Sue breathed the words.

Maggie tugged on Sue's hand. "Please, can Dr. Nelson see Daddy?"

"For Valina's sake?" Dr. Nelson raised his brows.

Sue laughed through her tears. "By all means. For Valina's sake!" She turned and led him into the room.

Dr. Nelson stopped the girls from following. "Ladies, you had best stay out here. I might have to give him a shot, and sometimes I get a little wild with the needle."

"Well, I ain't going in, then." Ruby crossed her arms.

"I am not going in," Opal corrected.

"I didn't say you had to." Ruby glared.

Maggie was so relieved that their bickering made her laugh.

"If you think it's funny, you go in," Ruby challenged. "Maybe you'll get shot."

"Forget it, Ruby! I'm not going in there, either," Maggie told her.

"If we're real quiet, we could maybe hear what Dr. Nelson has to say," Opal suggested.

"You want to hear Daddy get a shot?" Ruby was horrified.

"No, I just want to hear what Dr. Nelson says about Daddy."

"No! We are not going to listen. That never turns out well," Maggie said. "We'll wait and let them tell us when they get good and ready."

It seemed like Dr. Nelson was in the bedroom forever. When he finally came out, Maggie had chewed her fingernails down to the quick.

"It was a good thing you girls weren't in there." He rolled down his sleeves. "I had to give your daddy three shots."

Opal whistled. "Three shots!"

Ruby groaned. Maggie searched Dr. Nelson's eyes for the secret.

"Maggie, I think your daddy will be fine. He needs medicine, rest and prayers."

"What's wrong with him?" Maggie spoke quietly.

"Dust pneumonia."

"Dust pneumonia?"

Dr. Nelson nodded. "He got tons of dust in his lungs. That causes infection to set in. Those shots and the medicine I'll

send with Valina will help him."

"Will he be okay?"

"Your daddy is a strong man. I think he was just too weak from the salt mine cave-in, or he never would have gotten caught out in the storm. He thought he could get Lulubelle out of the pasture and into the barn before it hit. Under normal circumstances, he probably could have, but not in the condition he was left in when he came back from Hutchinson."

"He's not going to die?"

"He's a strong man, Maggie, and he's a fighter. With God's help, I think he'll come through on the best end of the stick."

"Promise?"

"I wish I could promise, Maggie. You'll have to talk to God about that." Then Dr. Nelson knelt down on one knee and tipped her chin up with a gentle finger. "Sue told me you've been a trooper of a nurse. That has probably pulled your daddy through so far. You just keep it up, and I know he'll make it."

Maggie cried. The weight of the last four days lifted. She thought that if her arms had been wings, she would fly clear to the sun. Then she felt a warm surge of pride. Sue had told Dr. Nelson that Maggie was a good nurse.

"Can I go see him?" Maggie held her breath.

"You bet you can!"

Maggie barreled to Daddy's room. At the door, she skidded to a halt and turned. "Thank you, Dr. Nelson."

Sue came out as Maggie went in. "Dr. Nelson, I'm so sorry that we can't pay you."

Dr. Nelson pointed to the empty space where Maggie had stood. "That was pay enough."

CHAPTER 5

That Mrs. Crenshaw

aggie didn't know how it had been decided that she would go with Valina for Daddy's medicine, but it was good to be in the wagon and riding away from the boxcar house. The sun sprinkled through the straw brim of Valina's hat, speckling her face with a delicate print of light and shadow.

"Martin's waving his Hoover flag again," Valina chuckled.

"Hoover flag?"

"Yes, ma'am."

"What is a Hoover flag?" Maggie asked.

"Hmm." Valina thought for a moment before she tried to explain. "Well, you know that Mr. Herbert Hoover is our President. Mostly, he is getting the blame for this here depression and no money and no jobs and no rain, and even for all these dust blizzards."

"President Hoover is causing all these terrible things?" Maggie widened her eyes in disbelief.

"No, no, Missy. All that is out of his hands. In fact, I reckon

that if he could fix them, he sure would. Then everyone would think he was some kind of hero."

"If it isn't his fault, why do people blame him?" Maggie wanted to know.

"Because he is the President. People feel better if they can blame someone. Just think about it, Missy. If the fault belongs to someone else, it does not belong to you. The President is a person everyone knows. He's in charge of the country, so he gets the blame. That is politics. The President carries the whole load on his shoulders," Valina explained.

"I wouldn't want to be President." Maggie made a sour face.

"Me, neither."

"Well, if everyone is against President Hoover, why are they waving a Hoover flag?" A puzzled look settled on Maggie's face.

Valina's rich laughter filled the air. "A Hoover flag is an empty pocket turned out of a man's britches. It shows that he doesn't have a cent to his name, and he is blaming President Hoover for it."

Maggie giggled. "I guess we have a Hoover flag, too!"

"More than half the country does, Missy." Valina pulled up in front of Dr. Nelson's office. "Miss Maggie, you jump down and fix these horses to the hitching post for me."

Maggie jumped, tied the horses and turned to wait for Valina. She took a deep breath. The air still had a dusty smell. She thought it might smell that way forever.

Valina joined her, and together they went into Dr. Nelson's office. "Miss Maggie, you ring that little bell so Dr. Nelson will know that we are here."

Maggie gave the bell a shake. Then she and Valina waited, sitting across the room from an older gentleman. Maggie watched as he folded a paper and tapped it across his knees. "Morning, Valina."

"Good morning to you, Mr. Giesick." Valina smiled.

"You've got quite a young lady there!" He put his forefinger to his eyebrow in greeting.

"Mr. Giesick, this is Miss Maggie Daniels."

"Oh, yes. Isn't your daddy the gentleman who married Sue?"

Maggie nodded.

"Welcome to Dodge City, Miss Maggie." He reached out a hand for her to shake.

Maggie shook hands. His hand felt strong and reassuring. She liked him.

Mr. Giesick tapped the paper. "Maybe you knew this family. As far as I can tell, they must have lived in the same area as your daddy's farm." He opened the paper to show Maggie the headline, "Dust Storm Claims Three Lives."

Maggie blinked. Slowly, she took the paper and read, "As of yet, no names are being released. The bodies of three boys were found in one of two beds of the one-room house. It looked as if all three were peacefully at rest, until questionable marks were found on their throats. When a search was made, the mother's body was found half-covered in a dust drift about two miles down the road from the house. When questioned, the father would only comment, 'She said these dust storms were driving her crazy.'"

Maggie dropped the paper. This was someone in her area? A sick feeling swept through her as she looked down at her overalls. They were hand-me-downs—that was how she had gotten most of her clothes for the past three years. Could they have belonged to the boys down the road? She had played with those boys, explored with them and fought with them. Could dust storms sift into your mind and cloud things? Had they crept into the boys' mama's mind and done that? Please, Lord, don't let it be them! Maggie grabbed her stomach. Her world began to tumble.

A nurse opened the door to the waiting room and stood back as a patient stepped out ahead of her. Maggie looked up and sucked in her breath. It was Mrs. Crenshaw. She was the woman who had said Sue would be saddled with Maggie. She was the one who had slapped the newspaper on the kitchen table so they would know Maggie's daddy had been in the salt mine cave-in, and he was most likely dead. Mrs. Crenshaw was the one person Maggie didn't want to see. Maggie dropped her gaze to the floor.

Mrs. Crenshaw walked over to her, scanned her from top to bottom, stuck her finger under her chin and raised her face. "Overalls! You're that ragamuffin spitfire Sue took in, aren't you?"

Maggie twisted her chin free. "She married my daddy."

"Oh, yes. He has dust pneumonia, doesn't he? Dr. Nelson was saying he didn't know if your daddy would make it through the week or not." Mrs. Crenshaw held her lips in a grim line.

A hot fire seemed to surge through Maggie. She knotted her hands, but before she could do anything Valina stepped between the two.

"Mrs. Crenshaw!" Valina reached down and grabbed Maggie's clenched fist. "Just what are you trying to do to this poor child?"

Maggie tugged to get her hand away from Valina's. She

wanted to run somewhere and hide. Her heart was exploding, and she didn't want it to happen in front of that Mrs. Crenshaw woman. Maggie was afraid that woman would be happy if she died.

Maggie had liked Dr. Nelson. He had told her he thought her daddy had a good chance of making it. He had almost promised. Was he just saying that? Was he just trying to make her feel better? She had to get out of here, but Valina wouldn't let go.

Valina faced Mrs. Crenshaw and let her deep voice take charge. "Mrs. Crenshaw, I'm sure you must have misunderstood Dr. Nelson. He thinks Miss Maggie's daddy is very strong and has the will to fight this dust pneumonia and win. He told us to come and get medicine. With this medicine, Miss Maggie's daddy is going to get well."

Mrs. Crenshaw sniffed. "I suppose he is one of the strong ones. His kind usually are. Who is going to pay for this medicine?"

"That is none of your business." Valina drew nose to nose with Mrs. Crenshaw.

"It certainly is. I am a taxpayer—which is more than some people I know!"

Maggie had had it. Even though Valina still held her hand tight, her tongue was free. "Someday, maybe you will wave a Hoover flag!" she yelled.

Mr. Giesick laughed. Valina dropped Maggie's hand.

Mrs. Crenshaw stooped to look Maggie in the eye. "You … you spitfire! Someone needs to teach you some manners."

"You need to learn some, too!"

"Miss Maggie, that's enough," Valina ordered.

"More than enough!" Mrs. Crenshaw stood royally and walked to the door. Then she stopped and turned. "Someone had better take on the job before it's too late. Mark my words!" She slammed the door behind her.

"Young lady," Mr. Giesick laughed, "I've been waiting a long time for that to happen. That was priceless! If you are a chip off the old block, I'll bet your daddy is going to get well in record time."

Maggie tipped her head, searching for understanding.

"Mr. Giesick, Dr. Nelson will see you now," the nurse called.

He paused on his way to the door where the nurse stood. With an echo of a chuckle, he spoke. "It has been a pleasure to meet you, Miss Maggie Daniels."

"Eugene, is that you?" Dr. Nelson came to the door. "So, you aren't feeling up to snuff?"

"I'm much better now. Miss Maggie Daniels is quite a doctor herself. A bit of laughter cures much. What is that verse in the Bible? 'A merry heart doeth good like a medicine.' The good Lord sure knew what he was talking about."

Valina smiled. "He sure does."

Dr. Nelson's kind smile lit his face. "Well, hello, Maggie. It's good to see you. And how's your daddy?"

Maggie's eyes narrowed as she sized him up. Was he just making her feel good? Did he think her daddy was going to die?

"Maggie, is he okay?" Dr. Nelson looked worried.

Maggie swallowed. "Dr. Nelson, I just want to know one thing. Were you telling me the truth when you said that you thought my daddy would get well, or were you trying to make me feel better?"

All eyes looked to the doctor for his answer.

"Maggie, I would do anything in my power to make you feel better, but I would never give you false hope. I truly believe that your daddy is going to get well. His will alone has taken him through things most men would give up on. Maggie, he loves you and wants to be able to take care of you and his new family. I really believe that love will carry him through."

Maggie searched his eyes. "Mrs. Crenshaw said that you didn't think my daddy would make it through the week."

Dr. Nelson rubbed his hand over his chin before he carefully chose his answer. "Maggie, Mrs. Crenshaw sometimes misunderstands things that are said. She is a bit on the dramatic side, so she feels she must make plain events a little more juicy. I did not tell her that I didn't think your daddy would make it."

Valina was the one who convinced Maggie. "She's been doing that dramatic stuff all her life. She puts on airs. I guess it's because she was raised in the Gatlin house."

"She's a Gatlin?" Maggie asked.

"Shoestring," Mr. Giesick said.

"Shoestring?"

"That means distant. Cousin, I think," Mr. Giesick explained.

Maggie swallowed. Her daddy was a cousin, too. He was a cousin on the poor side. What if Daddy and Mrs. Crenshaw were cousins? That would mean she was related to that Mrs. Crenshaw woman. Maggie groaned.

"Related or not, I sure would have liked to stuff a sock in her mouth today." Valina shook her head. "Telling this poor child that!"

Mr. Giesick laughed. "I guess Maggie stuffed it in her mouth for you. I have never seen that woman so shocked in her life. She almost didn't know what to say."

Dr. Nelson joined in the laughter. As he calmed down, he told them, "Don't be too hard on Mrs. Crenshaw. Her life is about to change. She told me that two of her nephews are coming in on the train today. They are going to be staying the rest of the summer, because her sister is having complications with her pregnancy. It seems that her sister's doctor has ordered bed rest."

Valina whistled. "Mrs. Crenshaw is going to have children in her house? The good Lord sure does have a sense of humor—or maybe those boys are being judged!"

"I sure wouldn't want to be one of those boys," Maggie whispered. She felt as though little fingers had slid to her tummy and twisted it. Maggie was glad Daddy had married Sue. What would have happened to her if Sue had been like Mrs. Crenshaw? Maggie would never have been able to call Mrs. Crenshaw Mama. Quickly, she slid her hand into Valina's. She needed to feel something warm. Maybe that would settle her insides.

"Let me get you that medicine, ladies." Dr. Nelson reached over the counter, grabbed the brown bag and handed it to Valina. "I wrote the instructions down for you, Valina. If you have any questions, let me know."

"Thank you, Dr. Nelson." Valina turned to Maggie. "Shall we get this medicine to your daddy?"

Maggie nodded. She was tired of Dodge City. It seemed like every time she came here, she ran into that Mrs. Crenshaw woman. Maggie could do without that—maybe for the rest of her life.

As she and Valina stepped outside, she heard Mr. Giesick say, "That little girl is something else! Edward, if you need money to help on that bill, you let me know. I'll work something out."

In the wagon, Valina's deep, rich voice was gentle. "Miss Maggie, you need to watch that temper of yours. God doesn't give us permission to lose it. He tells us to be angry and sin not."

"How can you do that?"

Laughter rippled through Valina. "It takes the good Lord's help and a lot of self-control. Most people seem to be lacking in both. He also tells us to heap coals of kindness, and then He will take care of our enemies."

"She feels like an enemy."

"Then you start heaping those coals of kindness, and let God take care of her, Miss Maggie."

CHAPTER 6
Dreams

"**G**et to the cellar!"

Maggie was terrified. Mrs. Crenshaw's hair floated wildly about her head, as if it were under water. She had on a gray, silky gown that seemed to breathe on its own. Wind whipped the skirts of her gown and pulled at the skin of her face.

"I told you to get to the cellar, you ragamuffin spitfire!"

Maggie trembled. She didn't know if she was more afraid of the cellar or Mrs. Crenshaw. She couldn't move. She watched as Mrs. Crenshaw raised a knotted wooden cane over her head in slow motion. "I'll teach you some manners, one way or another!" the woman yelled.

Maggie turned and ran down dirt steps that had been chopped out of the earth. At the bottom, she tripped and fell head first. She lay there, trying to calm her heart, while her eyes adjusted to the dark. She listened to see if Mrs. Crenshaw would follow. Then she rolled over to get up and froze. Beside her was a hill of sifted dust. Sticking out of the dust like a dead

tree was an arm with a clawed hand. As Maggie stumbled to get up, the head of the neighbor lady from down the road—the one with the three boys—shot out of the dust heap. Maggie tried to scream, but no sound came. She drank great gulps of air. The cellar shook as the door blasted shut. Maggie was swallowed in darkness. She kicked, belching forth the screams that would not come earlier.

"Maggie! Maggie!"

Somewhere, someone was shouting her name, but she didn't know who. She couldn't see in the dark cellar. Could it be the neighbor who had gone crazy? Was she calling for Maggie? If she was, what did she want with her? Maybe it was that Mrs. Crenshaw woman. Maggie wanted to find a corner to hide in, but she was afraid of what she might find in the corners.

"Maggie! Maggie!"

Someone grabbed her. Maggie stiffened.

"Maggie." This time the voice was soft. Maggie stopped screaming.

"Maggie. Margaret Pearl?"

Maggie relaxed.

"Honey, you are here with Ruby, Opal and me. Your daddy is in the other room. Maggie, just peep those eyes open and you'll see us," the gentle voice said.

Maggie's breathing slowed. A warm hand stroked her brow. Slowly, she opened her eyes. She knew who she would find, and she was right. She smiled through the worry that blanketed her eyes. Opal and Ruby were piled in the far corner of the bed. Maggie was tangled in the sheets.

"You were having a dream, Maggie," Sue told her.

Opal shuddered. "It was a nightmare."

Ruby's voice shook. "It was so bad that I thought I was having the nightmare!"

Maggie swallowed. "It was a very bad dream." She thought she could still feel the cold, dusty cellar and the icy eyes of Mrs. Crenshaw.

"Do you want to talk about it?" Opal asked.

"No, she doesn't. If it scared her that much, I don't want to hear it, and I sure don't want to dream it." Ruby shook her head.

"Ruby, that's silly. You can't dream someone else's dream," Opal told her.

"Girls, Maggie may feel like talking about it in the morning, but not right now." Sue looked to Maggie. "How about some warm milk?"

Maggie nodded, relieved that she didn't have to talk about her nightmare. Milk would be good.

"Milk in the night?" Opal was shocked.

"Yes, Opal, in the night."

"Like a tea party!" Ruby clapped her hands and ventured away from the wall for the first time since she'd been awakened by Maggie's cries.

"Yes, ma'am. Like a tea party." Sue smiled. "Ruby, you go get the teacups. Opal, you warm a little milk. I'll bring Maggie."

Opal and Ruby tumbled to the door. Sue waited for Maggie. "Maggie, are you all right?"

Maggie shuddered. "Mmm. I think I will be, but I never want to have that dream again."

"I hope you never do." Sue paused. "Maggie, when you want to talk about it, I'm here. If you never want to talk about it, that's okay, too."

Maggie nodded. She got up, and Sue wrapped a quilt around her. Maggie's body wasn't cold, but inside she could still feel the chill of the cellar. She was glad for the quilt.

The three girls snuggled on the bench behind the table. Sue pulled up her rocker. In no time, Opal and Ruby were giggling. Maggie took a gulp of milk and felt the warmth slide all the way down. She shivered.

Ruby pointed. "That means a ghost walked over your grave."

Opal jabbed her. "You dummy! You don't tell someone who has just had a bad dream that a ghost is walking over their grave."

Ruby glared. "Maggie knows I wasn't thinking when I said that."

"That's your trouble. You never think."

"And I 'spose you do?"

Maggie laughed. It felt good to hear Opal and Ruby bickering.

Sue smiled. "Girls, I think you should both grow up to be lawyers. The arguing that you do will make you great in the law profession."

"Is this just a girls' party, or can anyone join?"

"Daddy!" Maggie let the quilt drop from her shoulders and ran to his side.

Daddy leaned against the wall. His sunken eyes sparkled. Maggie thought she had never seen such a wonderful sight. "I wish that Mrs. Crenshaw woman could see you now!"

"I'd rather not see a soul until I've had a good long bath and a shave. Mrs. Crenshaw? Just who is she?" Daddy walked to the table and sank into a chair.

"She's the lady who brought the ham when you married Mama. You've got to remember her! She is always talking, Daddy." Opal padded on bare feet to stand beside his chair.

"And mostly, she says nothing good." Ruby joined Opal at his side. "Can I sit on your lap?"

Maggie closed her eyes to fight the strand of jealousy as it tightened around her heart. She wanted to be the one beside Daddy. If anyone was going to sit on his lap, it should be her.

"No. You may not sit on his lap. He is not quite strong enough to hold big girls like you two," Sue told them.

Maggie was glad.

"Maggie had a real scary dream," Opal explained.

Ruby poked out a pouting lip, until she saw the attention Opal was getting with her comment about Maggie's dream. Then she joined in. "It wasn't a dream. It was a nightmare."

"And she almost killed Ruby and me," Opal added.

"Oh? Then I am sure glad you woke her up. Let's see, are there any battle scars? Broken bones? Bruises?" Maggie's daddy teased.

"No, but that's because we woke her up," Opal explained.

By this time, Maggie was giggling. She loved to watch Daddy tease, and Ruby and Opal fell for anything he said. She smiled as she realized that she wasn't jealous of the girls this time.

Peace settled inside Maggie. Daddy was so much better that she believed Dr. Nelson with her whole heart. Daddy was going to be fine. He didn't have that hacking cough, and his fever was gone. Maggie tapped her fingers in her palm, counting the days since he had been taking the medicine. It had only been a little more than a week. She watched as Daddy tickled the bruise Opal claimed to have. She wished Mrs. Crenshaw could see him. It would show her! Maggie hadn't told any of the family what Mrs. Crenshaw had said. It had hurt and worried her so much that she didn't want anyone else to go through those horrible feelings about Daddy not making it. Daddy had made it throughout the week, when Mrs. Crenshaw had said he wouldn't.

"Yes!" she said out loud.

"Maggie? You do see a bruise?" Daddy held Ruby's arm high to examine it. "Maybe you'd better show it to me." He laughed.

Maggie smiled. The only bruise she knew of was one that couldn't be seen. It was deep in her heart. With Daddy getting better, the bruise was going away.

Sue stood up from the table and gathered the empty cups. "Back to bed, ladies."

The girls protested with moans, groans and a few yawns, but Sue won. They traipsed toward their room. As Maggie was about to follow Ruby and Opal through the doorway, Daddy called her.

"Maggie, come here a minute."

"Yes, Daddy?"

"Come sit on my lap."

Maggie looked to Sue to see if it was all right.

Sue nodded. "For a little bit."

There was no place Maggie would rather be. Gently, she eased herself onto his lap. Daddy wove his arms about her. She leaned on his chest. She could feel his heartbeat.

"Maggie, Sue and I have been talking. She feels I need to tell you that I am going back to Hutchinson, to the salt mines."

Maggie stiffened.

Daddy felt the movement and brushed her hair with his hand. "Maggie, I know they will give me my job back, and I have to have a job."

Still Maggie kept silent.

Sue came to the table and sat close. "Maggie, your daddy promised he wouldn't go until Dr. Nelson said that he was well enough."

"When?" Maggie asked.

"Soon, I hope," Daddy told her.

"Maggie, I don't think it will be for a few more weeks. Your daddy isn't strong enough yet. I know Dr. Nelson won't release him until he thinks your daddy will be fine," Sue said.

"It's got to be as soon as possible." Daddy ran his fingers through his hair. "I've been out of work for more than a month, and I've got to support my family. We can't live on nothing."

Maggie could see how troubled Daddy was. In her whole life, she had never known him not to work. Still, she didn't want him to go. "What about a job here?" she asked hopefully.

"I tried that. There were none."

"But now maybe there would be."

"Why, Maggie?"

Maggie clutched his hand. "The newspaper, Daddy. Remember? It told how you had tried to save the men you worked with, and how you had been buried alive for five days."

"Because the newspaper called me a hero? Because I've been hurt? It would be a charity job, Maggie, and there wouldn't be much money in that." He shook his head. "No. It's got to be the salt mines. And," he paused, "it's got to be soon."

Maggie couldn't help the tears. Daddy didn't seem to mind them. This stupid depression! This stupid drought with all its dust blizzards! They had changed her life so much. Mama was gone, and now these things were taking her daddy away. She wished they'd been something she could touch, so she could fight them, but how could you slug a dust storm or a depression? They were so much bigger than she ever hoped to be! No wonder the neighbor lady had gone crazy. She had probably thought she was saving her boys a ton of grief—or, maybe, by killing them herself she thought she was beating the depression and the dust blizzards.

Sue handed Maggie a handkerchief. Maggie noticed that she, too, was crying.

"I don't like it, either," Daddy said, "but I am not going to give up. I am going to do whatever I can to keep this family afloat. Maggie, I am doing it because I love you and Sue and the girls. I don't know if you can understand this, but it is because I love you."

Maggie nodded. She didn't doubt that Daddy loved them.

Sue stroked Maggie's cheek. "Honey, you have such a special daddy! He will do anything in his power to keep us going. You should be very proud of him."

Maggie was proud of him, but she was scared, too. "The last time he went, he almost got killed," she whispered.

"Maggie, he almost got killed here in the dust storm." Sue was gentle. "Your daddy and I have talked about it and prayed about it, and we feel that this is what the Lord would have him do. Maggie, we have to put your daddy in God's hands. They are bigger and better than ours."

Maggie sniffed and finally nodded. She slid off Daddy's lap, hugged his neck and trudged to her room.

She crossed to the window to watch the night sky. Up there, somewhere, lived the God of her heart. How He could be up there and in her heart at the same time was a mystery.

"Dear God in my heart, I guess Daddy is waving a Hoover flag. He says he's got to go back to the salt mines. I don't want him to go, but his mind is set in stone. Sue said to put my daddy in your hands because they are bigger than ours, so that's what I'm doing. Please take care of him, and please, please bring him back."

Maggie stood at the window and watched the wind sweep dust across the face of the moon. It was a long time before she crawled into bed beside Opal and Ruby.

The Job

*P*astor Olson's deep voice carried through the little wooden church. "He maketh my feet like hinds' feet, and setteth me upon my high places."

Maggie tipped her head and tapped her daddy's arm. "What are hinds?" she whispered.

"Mountain goats and deer, and animals like that," Daddy answered.

Maggie looked down at her feet. God makes our feet like goats' feet? That was something she didn't understand. She wasn't sure she wanted her feet to be like goats' feet.

"Ooh!" Opal pulled her feet up onto the pew and sat on them.

Pastor Olson smiled. "It doesn't mean that God will turn our feet into mountain-goat feet. It is a picture that God paints for us. Have you seen the calendar at the Co-op feed store?"

There were nods. Someone at the back blurted out, "Oh, yes!"

"I love that calendar. In fact, I asked Mr. Nolan if I could have it at the end of the year. I think he said that I could just because he was tired of me coming into his store, pulling it off the wall and looking through it."

Chuckles arose from the pews.

"Even though that calendar is only black and white, it portrays magnificent beauty, showing places where mountain goats climb. These goats are at the top of some of the most majestic mountains I have ever seen. The goats have no problem getting there, and very seldom do they fall. They live at the top of those rugged, craggy, rocky mountains. God is telling us that if we put our hand in His, we can make it through the ragged passages of life and live at the top of those mountains. Folks, that is victory in the Lord. That is where I want to live!"

Living at the top of mountains! That would sure beat the horribly dry, dirt-storm farmland around here. Maggie shook her head. Pastor Olson had said to put your hand in God's hand. Sue had said to put Daddy in God's hands. Just how big were God's hands, anyway? They must be gigantic, miracle hands. Miracle hands! Maggie hoped they were. She needed a miracle because Daddy would be leaving in a few weeks. Something just had to happen before then, or Daddy would be back in the salt mines.

Maggie closed her eyes tight. "Dear God in my heart," she mouthed without making a sound, "I need a miracle. Daddy needs a job right here, so he won't have to go back to those old salt mines. I know you can work things out even if I don't know how you plan to do it. Please, please, please! Amen." She popped her eyes open and felt the warmth of peace spread through her. It made her feel better to pray.

Maggie looked at Opal to see if she had noticed, but Opal was watching something else. Maggie followed her gaze.

Across the aisle sat Mr. and Mrs. Crenshaw with two boys tucked beside them. They must be the nephews Dr. Nelson had spoken about. Maggie studied the situation. Mrs. Crenshaw looked different from usual. Her hat was cockeyed, her hair randomly spewed out under the brim. Her collar was rolled where it wasn't supposed to be, and she held a handkerchief to dab her eyes every now and then.

Maggie examined the boys a little more closely. The younger boy must be about the same age as Opal, or maybe a year older. The other one looked to be as tall as Maggie, so he must be about her age.

As she watched, the older of the two took something from his shirt pocket, held it in the palm of his hand and rolled it around. Finally, Maggie got a good view. The boy was holding the biggest June bug she had ever seen. A wicked smile crossed his face. He nudged his brother. Slowly, he eased his arm to the back of the pew and rested it behind his brother's back. He scanned the church to make sure no one was looking. Then, holding the June bug between his thumb and forefinger, he aimed and tossed. The June bug sailed a short distance and dropped down the gaping collar of Mrs. Crenshaw's dress.

Quickly, the boy pulled his arm off the back of the pew. His face turned red as he tried to stifle his laughter. He looked away. Maggie's mouth dropped open. Mrs. Crenshaw squirmed. With a whoosh, she shot up, clapped her hand over her mouth and ran from the building.

Pastor Olson stopped in mid-sentence. The congregation swiveled in their seats to stare at the open door.

Mr. Crenshaw looked like a lost puppy. He swallowed.

"Maybe I'd better go check on her." He followed his wife out the door. Everyone heard him ask, "What are you doing?"

"Something is in my dress!" she yelled.

"Quit dancing and hold still."

"I can't!"

"Yes, you can."

"It's biting me!"

"Well…" Pastor Olson tried to begin again, but the people were more interested in the conversation outside. "This would be a good time for an offering. Would a couple of men come forward? We'll pray."

Maggie never even heard the prayer or knew when the offering plate came around. She was twisted in her seat, trying to see the Crenshaws.

"It's just a June bug, dear," Mr. Crenshaw consoled his wife.

"I'm going to die!" she wailed.

"No, you won't die. June bugs aren't poisonous."

"I know that! I mean I'm going to die of embarrassment. I will never be able to look these people in the eyes again."

"Yes, you will. These people are the best. They won't think anything of it, dear."

"Let's go home before anyone comes out of the church," Mrs. Crenshaw ordered.

"Dear, remember the boys?"

Mrs. Crenshaw wailed. "How can I forget! I'll never understand my sister. After those two boys, why would she have another baby?"

The two boys jumped from their pew and tumbled over each other to get to the door. Maggie giggled. Ruby blinked. "I didn't know Mrs. Crenshaw could run."

Opal looked at Maggie. "Did you see what happened?"

"Yep!"

Maggie didn't know if Pastor Olson had dismissed the congregation or not, but everyone poured outside. Opal grabbed her hand, and they slipped through the maze of people to see what would happen next. Opal squeezed between two men and rammed into the older of Mrs. Crenshaw's nephews.

"Watch where you're going, squirt!"

"Squirt?" Opal's eyes shot fire.

"Yeah, squirt!"

"I saw what you did. I can tell Mrs. Crenshaw, so you'd better take that back."

"Oh, yeah? And just what did I do?"

"You flipped that June bug down the back of her dress. That's what you did, and that's what I'll tell her."

He shoved his face close to hers. "I'll tell her you're a liar, and she'll believe me because I'm her nephew."

Maggie stepped between the two. As she spoke to Opal, she kept her eyes on the boy. "Opal, come with me. Forget it."

"He called me a squirt." Opal held her ground.

"I don't care. Just come with me."

"You'd better listen to her, squirt," the boy chuckled. "It'll save you from getting beat up."

Maggie glanced across the people to see Mrs. Crenshaw watching her. A strange look had settled on Mrs. Crenshaw's face. It made Maggie feel unsettled.

Opal squirmed. Maggie grabbed her to keep her from diving into the boy. At the same time, she couldn't resist warning him through clenched teeth, "You're lucky I held her back. She's a maniac fighter. Next time, I'll let her have you."

"Sure she is!" He grabbed his belly and bent over laughing.

Ruby had been watching, and she had had enough. She barreled into the boy from behind and knocked him rolling. Then the three girls giggled and ran for the wagon. From there, they watched as he pulled himself from the ground. He held up a fist and shook it in the air.

"What was all that about?" Valina stood beside the wagon.

"That boy! He called me a squirt." Opal didn't care if the whole world knew. "Maggie wouldn't let me beat him up."

"You had best tell Miss Maggie thank you. Miss Opal, you don't have any business a'fightin' a boy, and certainly not in your Sunday-go-to-meetin' clothes." Valina shook her finger.

"He threw that June bug down Mrs. Crenshaw's dress. I saw him do it, and so did Maggie."

"Hmm." Valina shook her head. "Those two boys are a handful, all right. Mrs. Crenshaw has been having me go over and help her a bit since they stepped off the train, but I don't rightly know what to do. She don't know what to do with them, and they are running that household wild." Valina paused and let her deep, rich chuckle fill the air. "I don't rightly know just who is being judged, Mrs. Crenshaw or those boys."

Maggie wasn't quite sure what Valina meant, but before she could speak, Ruby asked, "What does a judge have to do with it?"

Valina laughed, but she didn't answer. "Here." She handed Maggie a package wrapped in an old newspaper. "Give this to Mrs. Sue. Martin said he was tired of ordinary cornbread. This is sweet cornbread. I baked a whole panful, and we ate on it a few days, so I thought you might take it off my hands."

Maggie took the package. She guessed it must have been a huge pan. "Thank you, Valina." Maggie knew how bare the

In the Shadow of the Enemy

cabinet at home had been growing, and there was no money. Potatoes and bread had been their meals for the last week. No one complained. Sue was a good cook, so she could think of gobs of ways to make potatoes.

"You enjoy them. Tell Mrs. Sue and her man hello for me, and if you need anything, you just ask."

"Yes, ma'am."

With a sigh, Valina turned away. "I just imagine Martin is getting a bit restless. I best head that way."

Daddy and Sue made their way to the wagon. "That was an unusual ending for Sunday morning service." Daddy helped Sue into the wagon.

"It sure was!" Sue laughed. "I didn't know Mrs. Crenshaw could move so fast."

"Pastor Olson was shocked when she jumped and ran," Daddy added.

"In all fairness, I might have done the same thing if a June bug fell down my back." Sue was still laughing.

"It didn't fall down her dress. That boy flipped it down her dress," Opal told them.

"Are you sure?" Sue asked.

"Yep. I saw him, and Maggie did, too."

Daddy laughed. "Boys will be boys."

"Oh?" Sue raised her eyebrows. "Then I am certainly glad we have girls."

"Valina brought us some cornbread. She said Mr. Martin was tired of it," Ruby told them.

"Sweet cornbread!" Opal rubbed her tummy. "If Mr. Martin is tired of Valina's cooking, he must not be in his right mind."

70

"Well, then I'm glad he's not in his right mind." Daddy winked and laughed.

"It will be a nice change. When we get home, Maggie, you take Opal and pull the milk out of the well house. Ruby, you can set the table. We'll have sweet cornbread and milk for dinner." Sue smiled.

"Sounds good to me." Daddy flipped the reins. Ben and Maude lumbered into action.

"Wait!"

Everyone turned around. Mrs. Crenshaw was running toward them, holding her hat on her head.

"Oh, no," Opal whispered. "That boy probably told on us."

"Wait!" Mrs. Crenshaw's skirts were flying.

Daddy pulled the horses to a stop.

Mrs. Crenshaw heaved, trying to catch her breath. "I … have … a … business … proposition … to … discuss … with you."

Daddy nodded.

Mrs. Crenshaw looked back to her husband for help, but he was busy with the boys. She took a deep breath and began, "I want to hire your girl."

"For what?" asked Daddy.

"Help. I need someone to help me. I talked to my husband just now, and he said he thought it was a good idea." Mrs. Crenshaw avoided looking at Maggie.

"What would she be doing?" Daddy asked.

"Oh, whatever—just whatever I need help with at the time. Maybe watching the boys…"

"No!" Sue came to Maggie's rescue.

"I know you can use the money, and I am willing to pay a dollar a day. That is a lot of money for someone her age."

"No," Sue answered again. "If you need help, I can come and work for you."

Mrs. Crenshaw shook her head. "I can't. Thomas won't let me."

"Thomas Gatlin?"

Mrs. Crenshaw nodded. "If anyone hired you or Mr. Daniels, I think Thomas would run them out of town. He owns the house we live in. Even though he has promised it to me, he would take it back. He's not in his right mind—he hasn't been, ever since you two married."

"Then the chances are that he would do the same if Maggie were to work for you," Sue told her.

"I don't know." Mrs. Crenshaw paused. "Really, he wouldn't even have to know. He would just think she was another child in the neighborhood. Besides, he seldom comes over."

Sue shook her head. "I don't think it is a good idea."

"I would like to try." Maggie spoke up quietly. Everyone turned to stare at her. "Please?" She looked at Sue and Daddy. They were silent. "We need the money, Daddy. We need it bad. I know I could do it."

What Maggie didn't say was that this might be the very job she had prayed for in services today. Wow! The God of her heart sure took care of things fast. Maybe Daddy wouldn't have to go to the salt mines.

Still Mrs. Crenshaw didn't look at Maggie. "She could come every morning, and she could go home every night."

"Please?" Maggie begged. She could see that Daddy was thinking about it. Sue was the one she would have to convince.

"I could get up early and do my chores."

Daddy looked to Sue.

Maggie watched Sue wiped a tear from her cheek. "Sam, I don't know."

"It would be a help," Daddy said gently.

"Yes! I could help." Maggie clapped her hands.

"But no weekends," Sue put in.

"And she comes home before dark," Daddy added.

"I'll agree to that. Your girl can start first thing tomorrow morning." Mrs. Crenshaw started to walk away, then stopped and turned back. "She is not to wear any of those overalls. That's men's clothes, and I don't want my nephews to be influenced badly."

"Mrs. Crenshaw, she only has one dress, and it's her Sunday dress. It is also something of her mother's. I will not let her work in it." Sue was firm.

Maggie could see that Mrs. Crenshaw wanted to argue, but she also wanted the help. She held up her finger. "One week. She'd better have something else to work in by then."

Mrs. Crenshaw turned, slid her hat into the proper position on her head and walked toward the boys, who were sliding down the rail of the church steps. "Quit that right now!" she yelled.

The boys continued to slide.

"I don't know." Sue spoke to Daddy in a low voice, but Maggie heard. "I don't know if she will be nice to Maggie."

Opal groaned. "Maggie is going to work for Mrs. Crenshaw?"

"Only if she is nice to Maggie," Sue told her.

"I don't know if she is ever nice." Opal crossed her arms.

"She ain't," Ruby added.

"Isn't," Opal corrected.

Maggie could only smile. Now Daddy wouldn't have to go to the salt mines.

CHAPTER 8

First Day on the Job

*M*aggie rolled over and gazed at the dusky light filtering through the window. It was the time of morning when the sleeping sun blanketed the land, just before it touched the eastern ridge of the sky. Maggie slipped her fingers over the edge of the quilt and stretched, as the sun gently awoke—its fingertips magically lighting the sky in pastel colors. Morning!

Maggie stretched. Then she remembered that this was the day of her new job. She tumbled out of bed, pulled open her dresser drawer and grabbed her overalls.

Her hands trembled. Just how would it be to work for Mrs. Crenshaw? How would it be to be with her all day? Sue wouldn't be there to help her in any way. Maggie would have to do it all alone. She smiled. No, she wouldn't be alone. The God of heaven lived in her heart, and that meant she didn't have to do anything alone.

"What are you doing?" Opal yawned.

"I'm getting ready to go to work, remember?"

Opal groaned. "Mrs. Crenshaw. That mean old woman!

Maggie, aren't you scared?"

Ruby yanked the quilt over her head and shuddered. "I am!"

Maggie laughed uneasily. "Yes, I am scared, but I am not going to let her know it."

"How can you not let her know it?"

"I am going to look her right in the eye every time she tells me to do something," Maggie told them, all the while hoping she could do it.

"I wouldn't look in her eyes. I think she is too scary." Ruby peeked from beneath the quilt.

"Evil! That is Mrs. Crenshaw." Opal scooted closer to Ruby.

"Girls!" Sue lifted the quilted door. "You will make Maggie afraid to go to work. Mrs. Crenshaw is not evil. She is just a lady who has never been taught how to be friendly and polite. You have, so you know you shouldn't be talking in this manner."

"But we weren't talking to her. We were just talking about her," Ruby explained.

"Well, you shouldn't be talking about her, either," Sue reminded them.

"Mama, we weren't making up stories about her. We were just saying how she is." Opal sat up in bed.

Ruby nodded. "Yep, she sure is scary."

Sue put her hands on her hips. "No more 'scary,' then."

"Yes, ma'am," the girls agreed.

"Breakfast is in five minutes, so you girls had better get dressed fast." Sue left.

Opal and Ruby threw off the covers and piled out of bed. "I still say that Mrs. Crenshaw is the scariest woman in all Dodge City, Kansas," Opal whispered. "Maybe in the whole world!"

"Opal!" Ruby warned.

"You better not tell."

"Then you'd better not be saying those things. Mama just said that we aren't to say what we think about mean old Mrs. Crenshaw." Ruby stood with both hands on her hips, just like her mama had done before.

Opal and Maggie laughed.

Maggie sat on the floor and shoved her finger through the hole in the toe of her shoe. The shoes were still too big, but the boys down the road had grown out of them, and there was a lot of wear left in them. She felt sad again for the boys. It surely must have been them in the newspaper. Their mama had always seemed so nice. Had she gone dust crazy?

"Maybe she is crazy," Opal said.

Maggie was startled. "What?"

"Mrs. Crenshaw. Maybe she is crazy," Opal repeated.

Maggie shuddered.

"Opal! Now you did scare Maggie," Ruby scolded.

"Breakfast!" Sue called.

The three girls bounded for the table, slipped into their places, and after grace was given they dove in.

Maggie played with her oatmeal. She just couldn't help thinking about the lady down the road and Mrs. Crenshaw. What if Mrs. Crenshaw was going crazy? At church yesterday, she hadn't looked or acted the way she usually did.

Daddy broke into her thoughts. "Maggie, eat your oatmeal."

"After breakfast, I'll walk you to work," Sue told her.

"What about my chores?" Maggie asked.

"All of us are going to pitch in and do them for you." Daddy smiled. "I'm going stir-crazy. I need something to do."

Maggie looked to Sue.

"It'll help your daddy. Fresh air is wonderful, and I think he is ready to do a few things around here." Sue smiled. Then she turned to Daddy and added, "He will take it slow and easy, though."

Daddy laughed. "Yes, ma'am."

Maggie didn't even have to help clear the table.

Sue took her cold hand. It wasn't cold because of the weather, it was cold with fear. Sue's hand felt warm and safe. Together, they went out the door and started on their journey.

"It is shorter to cross the Gatlin pasture, but since Mr. Thomas Gatlin put in those no-trespassing signs, we'll have to go the long way. The Crenshaws live on the other side of the Gatlins." Sue continued to talk as they walked. Maggie didn't feel much like talking.

They headed west across their own pasture, where Lulubelle watched them with a wary eye. "It's okay, Lulubelle. I'm not coming to get you to milk," Maggie giggled.

"This path cuts right behind Valina's place. If you ever need to stop for anything, Valina would be glad to help you. Just remember that their house belongs to Mr. Thomas Gatlin, and it is on his property. I don't think he would do anything about you being there, but I don't know that for sure."

Maggie was glad Mrs. Crenshaw's house was close to Valina's place. She nodded.

Valina rose from her garden with a handful of weeds. "Land sakes! Am I having visitors this early in the morning? Come on in."

Sue laughed. "Valina, I see you're hard at work already this morning."

"I'm trying to beat the heat, but I done think the heat

beat me." Valina laughed and wiped the back of her hand across her forehead. "I'm ready for a break. Come on in and have tea with me."

"We can't. We are on our way to Mrs. Crenshaw's. She's hired Maggie to work for her."

Maggie could hear the regret in Sue's voice. Maggie knew that Sue would rather have been the one Mrs. Crenshaw hired, but Maggie was glad of the job.

Valina paused. Maggie watched the woman's warm brown eyes search Sue's face. "Money's hard to come by these days."

Sue nodded. "Yes, it is."

Valina gently lifted Maggie's chin. "Missy, if you ever need anything, you run yourself over here. I'm just a stone's throw from the Crenshaw place."

"Yes, ma'am," Maggie agreed.

"Thank you, Valina." Sue put her hand on Valina's arm. "I really appreciate it."

"You know that anything you need, I'm willing…" Valina let the sentence hang unfinished.

Sue nodded. "Thank you, Valina. We'd better be on our way." Sue and Maggie headed around to the side of Valina's house. Maggie looked back. Still standing and watching them, Valina lifted her hand and waved.

In front of Valina's house stood the Gatlin mansion. Every time Maggie saw it, she was in awe.

"In this row of trees there is a side gate. Let's go that way, and not through the main gate." Sue led the way. Maggie thought it was because they had less chance of being seen.

The trees had grown over the gate until it was almost

hidden. Sue and Maggie had to push the gate to swing it open. The hinges creaked.

From the gate, they walked to the street. Sue pointed. "That is where the Crenshaw house is."

The long carriage drive was strewn with trees. The branches hung close. Maggie felt as if they were fingers reaching out to grasp her. When she entered the dark tunnel of trees, her back tingled as if eyes were following her. At the end of the dusty drive, she could see a tall house whose attic was adorned with shutters. She shivered. Attics were where old things were laid to rest. The house was big, but not nearly the size of the Gatlin mansion. Miniature pillars lined the porch, which stretched across the front and wrapped around one side of the house.

A hush fell upon Sue and Maggie as they walked up the drive. Maggie looked at the steps and paused. When she stepped on them, she would be entering another world. The steps were solid, but the paint was beginning to peel.

Together, Sue and Maggie went up the steps and crossed the porch. Maggie held tightly to Sue's hand while Sue knocked on the screen door. The front door behind it yawned wide open. Maggie could hear the footsteps on the wooden floor before she saw Mrs. Crenshaw.

"If I have told those boys once, I have told them a hundred times to keep this door closed." Mrs. Crenshaw pushed her hair back from her forehead. "Come in." She held the door open.

Maggie and Sue stepped inside.

"Sue!" Mrs. Crenshaw seemed surprised. "Thanks for bringing your girl. I'll send her home before it gets dark." She dismissed Sue.

Sue hesitated. Then she said, "Mrs. Crenshaw, my girl has a name. It is Margaret Pearl. Maggie for short."

Mrs. Crenshaw looked at Maggie for the first time. "Very well, then. Maggie." Still she seemed to be waiting for Sue to leave. The silence stretched. Maggie squirmed. A fly buzzed through the open screen door.

"You are letting the flies in." Mrs. Crenshaw spoke to whichever one of them wanted to listen.

Sue knelt beside Maggie. "Maggie, if you don't want to do this, I'll take you home right now." She kept hold of Maggie's hand.

Maggie swallowed. "I want to do it."

She knew it was a lie the minute it left her lips. She did want the job, so her daddy wouldn't have to go back to the salt mines, but she sure didn't want to stay with Mrs. Crenshaw. She eased her hand out of Sue's. "I'll be fine." Then she bent closer and whispered, "God that lives in my heart will stay with me."

Sue smiled. "Yes, sweetie. He'll be with you." She caressed Maggie's cheek, rose and stepped out the screen door. It slammed shut and the sound of Sue's footsteps faded across the porch. Maggie felt empty.

"Cecil! Elbert!"

Maggie jumped.

"Cecil! Elbert! You boys get in here this minute!" Mrs. Crenshaw yelled.

The house vibrated as the boys bolted down the stairs and slammed to a stop in front of Mrs. Crenshaw.

"Cecil, Elbert, this is Maggie. She is here to help me. There will be times when she is in charge of you. You will do what she tells you to do."

Cecil let his eyes sweep Maggie from top to bottom. "She's just a girl. She's a girl in overalls. I'm taller than she is. She's not going to tell me what to do."

"Cecil, you will listen to her," Mrs. Crenshaw warned him. "You are used to the city, and life here is different. Maggie has been raised in the country."

He glared at Maggie. "She looks like the country—dirty!" The moment Mrs. Crenshaw turned her back, he slammed his fist into his hand. Elbert stuck his tongue out.

Mrs. Crenshaw didn't notice the boys. "Maggie, follow me."

Maggie followed. They went into the kitchen. Maggie sucked in her breath. The sink board was loaded with a mountain of dirty dishes. She didn't know how anyone could own so many. There must be a fortune in dishes beside the sink.

"This is where I want you to begin. I will be starting dinner after a bit, and I need these dishes cleaned. There's a tub that you can heat water in." Mrs. Crenshaw pointed beside the stove. "I'll be upstairs if you need me." Then she turned and left.

Maggie took a deep breath and studied the disaster area. At least there was a hand pump beside the sink, so she wouldn't have to carry water. She took the tub and slid it under the pump.

"Ouch!" Something stung Maggie's cheek. She rubbed it with her hand and felt a welt.

From behind the kitchen door, stifled laughter exploded. Maggie knew before she even looked that she would find Cecil and Elbert. She sprang toward the door.

Cecil and Elbert tumbled over each other. "Run, Elbert!" Cecil yelled as he surged from the floor. They ran.

On the floor lay a beanie shooter. Maggie picked it up and stashed it in her pocket. "You snots! You're going to get it!" she promised as they slammed out the back door.

She took a deep breath and turned to face the dish mountain. This was going to be a long day.

CHAPTER 9 · *Hooligans*

"Maggie!"

Maggie pulled her hands out of the dishwater and wiped them down the legs of her overalls. This must be the tenth time Mrs. Crenshaw had called her upstairs while she was doing the mountain of dishes. Maggie trudged upstairs.

"Maggie!" Mrs. Crenshaw hollered again from the bedroom doorway.

"Yes, ma'am."

Mrs. Crenshaw heaved a disgusted sigh. "Girl, when I call for you I want you now, not ten minutes from now."

"Yes, ma'am." Maggie spoke more to the floor than to Mrs. Crenshaw.

"I want your voice to sound more..." she searched for a word, "more chipper than that." Mrs. Crenshaw tapped her toe.

Maggie lifted her head and looked directly at her boss. "Yes, ma'am."

"That's much better. Now, downstairs is a basket of sheets.

Bring it to me, and you can help me put the sheets on this bed." Mrs. Crenshaw turned from Maggie, dismissing her.

"Yes, ma'am." Maggie hurried down the stairs, found the basket and brought it back upstairs. Eleven. That was how many trips up and down the stairs she had made by now.

"Are those dishes done yet?" Mrs. Crenshaw asked.

"No, ma'am." Maggie wanted to add that they would have been done if Mrs. Crenshaw hadn't called her away so many times, but she didn't. She didn't want to make Mrs. Crenshaw mad or give her any reason to fire her.

"The dishes are not done?" Mrs. Crenshaw paused to show disapproval. "I don't know that you are going to be worth a dollar a day."

Maggie's heart pounded. What if Mrs. Crenshaw lowered her wages? That might mean Daddy would have to go to the salt mines. Maggie swallowed. She would have to work faster and hope Mrs. Crenshaw quit calling her away from the dishes.

When the bed was made, Mrs. Crenshaw waved her on with, "I hope you are done in time for me to fix dinner."

Maggie ran down the stairs. She tripped on the last step and sprawled across the floor. Slowly, she pulled herself up and looked at the stairs. Stretched from one side of the bottom step to the other was a thin piece of taut rope. She yanked it free and heard smothered laughter. She slipped to the window and looked out. Cecil and Elbert were doubled up, rolling on the porch. She marched to the door and threw it open. Before she could yell at them, they flew around the side of the house. She gritted her teeth. "Later!" she promised.

"You aren't in the kitchen yet?" Mrs. Crenshaw poked her head around the top of the stairs.

Maggie ran to the kitchen. She didn't bother to answer Mrs. Crenshaw. Maggie would probably get in trouble for that, too. She felt like pounding Cecil and Elbert. She didn't think it would hurt them to do a few chores around this house. It might even keep them out of so much mischief. She plunged her hands into the dishwater. It wasn't warm anymore, but then Mrs. Crenshaw had kept calling her away. Maggie smiled. Being mad did help her work faster. She'd have the dishes done in no time.

When the last dish was dried, Mrs. Crenshaw walked into the kitchen. "Good. You can help me fix dinner. Count out eight potatoes from the potato bin. Then you can wash them."

Maggie counted them, washed them, cut them up for potato stew and cooked them. She half listened to Mrs. Crenshaw complain about Cecil and Elbert.

"Those boys are hooligans! My sister must be out of her mind to have another child. You know that she's got another besides Cecil and Elbert. Melbern. Yes, another boy. She wanted me to take him, too, but I just told her no. Melbern is two, maybe three years old. I don't have any business with a child that young. He needs his mama."

Maggie thought Mrs. Crenshaw didn't have any business with children of any age, but she didn't say a word.

"I think my sister had two miscarriages between Elbert and Melbern, and trust me, they were probably boys, too. Maggie, go set the table. You can set four places, and hurry it up. Mr. Crenshaw will be home before long."

"Four places?" Maggie asked.

"Four places."

Maggie wondered if she was going to get to eat. Mrs. Crenshaw hadn't said anything about that. Maybe Maggie was to bring her own lunch. With that thought, her tummy rumbled. She sat the bowls on the table.

"Grab the butter and the salt and pepper shakers from the sideboard," Mrs. Crenshaw told her.

Maggie fingered the salt and pepper shakers. They were beautifully cut glass. Never had she held anything as delicate and fragile as this. Quickly, she slipped them into the pockets of the apron Mrs. Crenshaw had insisted she wear. She didn't want to drop and break them.

"Hey! She's stealing your salt and pepper!" Cecil yelled, pushing Maggie from behind.

"I am not!"

"We saw her, didn't we, Elbert? She stashed them in her pockets." Elbert nodded. "Just look in her pockets," Cecil sneered.

Mrs. Crenshaw came to stand in front of Maggie. "Let me see what's in your pockets, young lady."

Maggie's mouth dropped open. She didn't know what to say. Sure, the shakers were in her pockets, but would Mrs. Crenshaw believe that she was trying to steal them? Her stomach turned, but this time it wasn't from hunger.

Mrs. Crenshaw held her hand out to Maggie. "Now! I want to see what's in your pockets."

Maggie's fingers were cold as she reached into the pockets and pulled out the salt and pepper shakers. "I put them in my pockets so I wouldn't drop and break them. I was just going to carry them to the table."

"I don't believe her." Cecil stuck his face close to hers. "We watched her look at them, and we could tell she wanted them. Couldn't we, Elbert?"

Again, Elbert nodded.

"Margaret Pearl Daniels! No wonder Sue hired you out. You've probably been stealing from her, too." Mrs. Crenshaw yanked the shakers from Maggie's hands.

"I did not steal! I just didn't want to break them." Maggie was so mad that tears exploded from her eyes, and she didn't even know it.

Mrs. Crenshaw shook her head. "I'll give you one more chance, young lady. But if you so much as look like you are taking anything, I will send you packing."

Maggie wanted to shout. She wanted to defend herself, but somehow she knew it would be twisted into the lie that Cecil had thrown before Mrs. Crenshaw.

The front door closed. Mrs. Crenshaw turned and stepped out of the room. "It's about time you got home, Arnold. These children have been driving me up a wall."

Cecil and Elbert danced around Maggie. "We got you in trouble, we got you in trouble," they chanted.

Maggie slid her hands across her cheeks. She wanted to call them names, but if she did, she would be deeper in trouble than she was already. She ground her teeth together to keep from saying anything.

"Come on, boys! Wash up and head to the table," Mrs. Crenshaw ordered.

Mr. Crenshaw was the first to sit. He sat at the head of the table with his back to the kitchen window. Cecil and Elbert slid onto the bench that was against the wall, and Mrs. Crenshaw sat across from Mr. Crenshaw.

Mr. Crenshaw said grace. "Dear Lord, we thank thee for what we are about to receive. Amen."

Maggie stood in the middle of the kitchen floor. She didn't know what to do. She guessed she was just supposed to watch them eat. Her tummy growled.

"Maggie, bring us the bread," Mrs. Crenshaw ordered.

Mr. Crenshaw looked up from his bowl. "Aren't you hungry, Maggie?"

Maggie was afraid to answer.

"Have you already eaten?" he asked.

Maggie shook her head.

"Child, we have plenty. Go get a bowl and join us." Mr. Crenshaw smiled.

Mrs. Crenshaw cleared her throat. "She is hired help, Arnold. She will eat after we do. I will not have her sitting at the same table we sit at."

"What?" Mr. Crenshaw was shocked. At that moment, Maggie thought he was the nicest man on earth.

"I won't have it! I will not send our nephews home telling their mama they had to eat with the hired help." Mrs. Crenshaw glared across the table at Mr. Crenshaw.

"I don't agree, Louise." Mr. Crenshaw turned to Maggie. "You are welcome to join us."

Maggie saw that Mrs. Crenshaw's lips were tight and her eyes held fire. She could imagine how hard it would be to work with the woman if she sat down at this table. There was a part of her that wanted to sit down and make Mrs. Crenshaw share her table with the 'hired help,' yet she knew that if she did, Mrs. Crenshaw would send her packing the minute Mr. Crenshaw went back to work. Maggie needed this job.

"Thank you, but I'm not very hungry," she lied. Her stomach would probably never forgive her.

When dinner was over, Mrs. Crenshaw scolded Maggie, warning her that in order to keep her job she must remember that Mrs. Crenshaw, and not Mr. Crenshaw, was the one who had hired her. Maggie wished it had been the other way around. Mr. Crenshaw was much nicer.

Then Mrs. Crenshaw told her that after the dinner dishes were done, the boys were in Maggie's care. Mrs. Crenshaw was worn out and needed a rest, and she would be upstairs for an hour.

Maggie's mind fought Mrs. Crenshaw all through doing the dishes. She thought about things she wished she had said and things she might have gotten by with saying. She smiled as she thought of how Mrs. Crenshaw's face would have looked if Maggie had sat at the table. Mrs. Crenshaw seemed to think that hired help was next to trash. Maggie remembered Mr. Crenshaw. He was nice. How did he end up with Mrs. Crenshaw? That was a mystery she would like to know.

Finally, she folded her apron, hung it from the back of a kitchen chair and listened. The house was too quiet for the boys to be inside—unless they were hiding around some corner, trying to get her in trouble again.

She slipped out onto the porch and leaned against a pillar. The afternoon sun was hot, and very little breeze stirred. Leaves draped from the trees as if all their energy had been drained. Maggie felt wilted, too. This job was hard work, but the real work was getting along with Mrs. Crenshaw. Again she smiled, as she remembered Mr. Crenshaw inviting her to sit at the table. If she had sat down, Mrs. Crenshaw would have come unglued. Maggie almost wished she had done it just so she could have seen that.

Every time she turned around, she got in trouble for something that wasn't her fault. She sure would like for those two boys to get what they deserved, but she would probably get in trouble for that, too. She'd better go find them.

Maggie stepped off the porch and shaded her eyes. The boys weren't in front of the house. She walked around the house. No Cecil, no Elbert. Quietly, she stood. Maybe she would be able to hear them.

Nothing.

She headed for the barn. They were most likely hiding from her. She needed to be careful. It seemed as though every time they were out of her sight, they were planning some terrible thing to do to her. Their beanie shooter was still in her pocket. She gathered a few small stones, but discarded the delicious thought of using them on the boys. That would get her in trouble for sure.

The barn was quiet. She stood just inside the door, listening. Nothing. The sweet smell of hay reminded her of home and invited her to dive into the stack, but she was at the Crenshaws'. That wouldn't be acceptable. She looked up toward the loft and groaned. She didn't want to climb up there to look for them.

"Like a rodeo!"

Maggie heard Cecil. The boys were behind the barn. She went to the back door of the barn and stepped outside. Cecil was on top of the wooden fence that separated the pasture from the yard. Elbert was below him, climbing the fence.

"I'm going to make that cow mad, like the rodeo clowns do," Cecil said. He dropped inside the pasture.

Maggie gasped. Her hand slipped to her throat, because that was where her heart had jumped. Memories fell on her like a black cloud of thick dust. She couldn't breathe. All she could see was Mama wading out into the pond to rescue their bull. The bull had panicked, twisting and tangling Mama in the rope, and Mama had drowned.

Maggie choked, ripping the black cloud of memory away. Not again! She had to stop those boys. "Cecil! Elbert! Stop!"

The boys laughed and ignored her. In what looked like slow motion, Cecil was running toward the biggest bull Maggie had ever seen. The bull, brown with black splotches over his body, grazed peacefully.

Cecil yelled, "Hey! You old, stupid cow!"

The bull's head shot up. Drool stretched from his mouth clear to the ground. Still Cecil ran toward him.

Maggie shouted, "Get out of there before you get killed!" Tears she didn't know she had shed streamed down her cheeks.

Cecil stopped in his tracks and turned to face Maggie. "Stupid girl! Cows don't kill people."

"It's a bull, not a cow. He'll kill you. Please!" Maggie pleaded.

"Scaredy-cat!" Cecil taunted, his back to the bull.

"Look out, Cecil!" Elbert yelled as he scrambled back up the fence.

The bull snorted and dug his hooves in the dirt. Dust shot up and billowed about him. Cecil didn't move.

"Run, Cecil, run!" Maggie screamed.

Cecil was frozen in place, but the bull wasn't. Maggie had to do something. She could not stand by. Cecil would be mauled by that bull. She shouted, but he couldn't hear her above the snorting and bellowing of the bull. Maggie searched for what she could do. "Dear God in my heart," she begged, "help me!"

Her eyes landed on Elbert. He had dropped to safety, but his shirt had caught on the fence. Elbert had been so afraid that he'd slithered out of the shirt and left it fluttering there. It was red. Maybe that would work.

Maggie dashed over, grabbed the red shirt, climbed the fence and ran wildly toward Cecil. Cecil was still frozen. Maggie dove at him and sent him tumbling to the ground in a dust cloud.

"Run!" she ordered.

Cecil scrambled to his feet and ran. So did the bull—right after Cecil!

Maggie gasped. She had no time to think. She crossed in front of the bull, waving the shirt like a red flag. The bull staggered to a stop. Then he charged at Maggie.

Now the bull was between Maggie and the fence. Frantically, Maggie searched for a place to run. The trees were too far away. The windmill! She took off.

Through the pounding staccato of the bull's hooves, Maggie thought she could feel his breath on her. She dove beneath the bottom rung of the windmill and lay there, heaving for air. The mad bull slammed into the side of the structure, denting the leg of the windmill. Maggie scrambled to her feet. She swung to the ladder, which was still vibrating from the force of the bull's weight, and climbed. If she could just get out of his sight, maybe the bull would forget about her.

The bull rammed the windmill again and again. Maggie held so tight to the steel frame that she couldn't tell the difference between the bull's crashing against the windmill and her own heart's pounding. The bull backed up, pawed the ground and charged yet again. His snot flung through the air, the sun glinting on it in pastel colors just before it landed on her arm. Maggie wanted to wipe it off, but she dared not let go of the ladder. Instead, she struggled for a better hold and dropped the shirt. She watched as it floated down and landed on top of the bull's head.

The bull shook his bulky head and bawled, but the red shirt was caught on his horn. Tremors ran through his body, and he erupted in rage. He twisted, jumped, turned and dove into battle with the red shirt. He charged across the pasture, the shirt dancing from his horn.

This was her chance. Maggie dropped to the ground and ran for the fence. She tumbled over it and lay on the dusty ground, gasping for air. "Dear God in my heart!" she sobbed.

"There she is!" Elbert pointed. "She took my shirt."

Mrs. Crenshaw stood over Maggie, hands on her hips. "Do you want to explain this, young lady?"

Maggie wiped her hand over her face to sweep away the tears and pulled herself up. "Explain? I saved Cecil's life."

"Oh?" Mrs. Crenshaw tapped her foot.

"He got in the field with that horrible bull. The bull charged, so I grabbed Elbert's shirt and made the bull chase me." She was still gasping.

"And just where are the shirt and the bull now?" Mrs. Crenshaw wanted to know.

Maggie turned to look. The bull was galloping across the pasture, red shirt flying. "There!" she pointed.

Mrs. Crenshaw paused. "Well, that shirt will certainly come out of your wages." She turned and walked back to the house. "You might as well call it a day and head home," she called over her shoulder.

Cecil and Elbert stared at Maggie. This time, they didn't laugh. "You want us to walk you part of the way?"

Maggie shook her head. She had had enough of Cecil and Elbert for one day. She had had enough of Mrs. Crenshaw for a lifetime.

She stood and dusted her overalls. Without a backward glance, she walked around the barn, around the house, up the tree-strewn drive and to the street. She wrapped her arms about her sides to steady her rumbling heart and the torrent of memories that surged through her. The boys followed her. As Maggie's feet clicked on the bricks, she heard Elbert ask, "Do you think she will come back tomorrow?"

Maggie caught her breath. Tomorrow? Yes, she would be back. She was not a quitter. She was a fighter, and she had a lot to fight for.

Heaping Coals

*M*aggie could feel the eyes of Cecil and Elbert burning holes in her back. She would not turn around. She would not let them see her cry. This had been one of the worst days in her whole life.

She walked down the bushy row of trees to the gate she and Sue had come through that morning. Then she stopped in surprise. The brush that had earlier choked the gate had been cleared away. When she swung it open, there was no screeching sound from the hinges. Someone had oiled them.

Maggie stepped through the gate and closed it behind her. It was like closing the gate on a part of the day she would like to forget. She leaned against the fence. Tears tumbled over her cheeks, and she plopped down to bury her face in her arms. Mrs. Crenshaw was the worst person she had ever been around, and she had been with her all day. She felt like a little mouse under the shadow of a soaring vulture with no place to hide. Maggie trembled. Even now, she could feel the shadow of the enemy.

"Lord have mercy, Missy! What be the matter?" Valina leaned over and stroked her hair.

Maggie tried to talk, but only sobs came.

"You come with me, Missy." Valina held out her hand.

Maggie wiped her face on the sleeve of her shirt and took the warm, welcoming hand.

"I have just the thing. You come follow me to my kitchen, Missy." Valina led the way, but she didn't let go of Maggie's hand.

When Valina opened the door, an aroma poured into the air that made Maggie's tummy squeeze and growl in hunger. She looked at Valina to see if she had heard it.

"Land sakes, Missy! When's the last time you ate?"

"Early this morning, before Sue walked me over to the Crenshaws'."

"You didn't have anything to eat at the Crenshaws'?" Valina furrowed her eyebrows.

Maggie shook her head.

"They don't have any food? They got those boys to feed, and they don't have any food? I best be talking to Pastor Olson. Maybe he can get something together for them." Valina shook her head. "It sure is hard times for folks, but I never would have guessed the Crenshaws would be waving a Hoover flag. Why, he's a banker!"

"Mrs. Valina, they aren't waving a Hoover flag. There was food." Maggie spoke quietly.

Valina looked at Maggie with searching eyes. "Then why didn't you eat?"

"It was my fault. Mr. Crenshaw wanted me to sit at the table, but Mrs. Crenshaw told him I was hired help and I had to wait and eat whatever was left after they were done eating. They were getting mad at each other. I didn't want to start a fight, so I told them I wasn't hungry." She shrugged her shoulders.

"Mrs. Crenshaw wouldn't let you eat at the table?"

Maggie shook her head.

"Lord have mercy on that woman! I feel like killing her and telling the Lord she done died. Of course, you know I wouldn't, but of all the nerve! She beats all." Valina paced the kitchen floor.

"Mrs. Valina, she feels like my enemy," Maggie whispered.

"Enemy! That be a good word for her, all right. And enemies need to be taken care of." Valina nodded.

"Mrs. Valina, you can't do anything bad to her, because I think I know what is wrong with Mrs. Crenshaw."

Valina stopped pacing and stood in front of Maggie, waiting.

"I don't think Mrs. Crenshaw has God in her heart. So if she dies, she won't go to heaven."

Valina's mouth dropped. "Out of the mouths of babes, I declare! I guess if you're willing to give her another chance, I best be willing, too."

"Mrs. Valina, I don't like her, but Sue told me that God loves all of us. Maybe if Mrs. Crenshaw lets God into her heart, she will change. Then maybe we'll all like her."

Valina looked at Maggie. "Well, our God is a God of miracles. That would certainly be one." She turned to the sideboard. "I just pulled these two pies out of the oven. Mr. Thomas Gatlin do like his sweets. He tells me to make as much as I want. Bless him! Are you wanting to try a piece?"

"Yes, ma'am!"

Valina scooped a big hunk of apple pie into a dish and placed it in front of Maggie. "I'll get you a glass of milk to go with it." When Valina set the glass on the table, she sat down also. She drummed her fingers. "At least, you don't have to go back there."

Maggie dropped the fork on the plate. "Yes, I do."

"Missy, you don't need to be around that woman. Not the way she treats you." Valina leaned over the table to look straight into Maggie's eyes. "Mrs. Sue won't allow that. Sue loves you, and she won't let Mrs. Crenshaw do that to you."

"Mrs. Valina, I have to go back. It's a job, and we need the money real bad. If I don't go back, my daddy will hop a train to the salt mines. I don't want him to go. I just have to keep this job." Maggie laid her hands flat on the table.

"Missy, when Mrs. Sue and your daddy hear about what happened today, they won't let you go back."

Maggie swallowed. "Then they can't hear about it."

Valina took a deep breath, but before she could say anything, Maggie stopped her. She looked deep into Valina's eyes. "You are the only one who knows, besides the Crenshaws. Please, promise you won't tell Sue or my daddy. Or anyone!"

"Oh, Missy!" Valina shook her head.

"Please! I just have to keep this job. It's for our family."

Valina sighed and gave in. "Missy, it's against my better judgment, but I'll give you my promise. I don't like it, but I can't even tell Martin. He'll go shoot off his mouth at that woman. You girls done found a place in his heart. Why, when he found out you'd be using that old gate, he cut the brush away and oiled them hinges. It'll be hard keeping a secret from my man. I'll do it, though—unless she harms you in any way.

If she lays a hand on you, the promise flies out the window. Do you understand that, Missy?"

"Yes, ma'am." Maggie was relieved. "Thank you, Mrs. Valina."

Maggie could tell that Valina wasn't at peace with her promise. She kept drumming her fingers on the table. Then, with a huff of triumph, Valina paused and looked at Maggie.

"Missy, I got us an idea."

Maggie swallowed a bite of the delicious pie and looked at Valina questioningly.

"I would say that it is time to heap coals."

Maggie sat still, the fork halfway to her mouth. "What?"

"Not hot coals, although that would bring me pleasure right now." Valina looked up to the ceiling. "Forgive me, Lord!" She chuckled. "Don't He beat all! Now, Missy, we need to be heaping coals of kindness. That's what the good book tells us to do. We heap coals of kindness on our enemies. Then their hearts make a change."

"How?" Maggie asked.

"It be one of His mysteries. But rest easy. If He says it will work, it will work." Again, Valina looked up somewhere past the ceiling.

"What do I need to do?"

"Missy, tomorrow morning you stop here on your way to the Crenshaw place. I'll send that other apple pie with you. Don't tell the Crenshaws I made it unless they ask. You just take it to them."

"Do you think it will work?"

"It's what the good Lord tells us to do, so we got to think it will work. Apple pie with prayer has got to get the ball rolling, at least."

Maggie smiled. All the hurt that had busted up her insides today had been eased away. Valina had a way of making her feel better. "Thank you, Mrs. Valina."

Valina stood and opened her arms, inviting a hug. The invitation didn't have to be given twice. Maggie stood, rounded the table and was swept into a hug. It felt like snuggling into quilts on a cold night. It reminded her of Mama.

Valina walked her to the door and watched her leave. Maggie knew she'd keep watching until she was out of sight. Those eyes on her back felt good. Not like Cecil and Elbert's! Valina's rich voice broke out in song. "When shadows surround us…"

Shadows … the shadow of the enemy seemed further away now, and Maggie had a plan. With Mrs. Valina's help, she would heap coals of kindness, starting tomorrow. "Thank you, God in my heart." Maggie looked to the sky and twirled around to wave one last time at Mrs. Valina, her friend.

At home, Opal and Ruby were waiting for her. They scrambled off the porch and ran her way. "How was your job?" Opal wanted to know.

Maggie giggled. "I'll bet you had more fun here."

"What did you do?" Ruby asked.

"Dishes! A mountain of dishes, and I did them twice."

"Ooh!" Ruby frowned.

"Did her sister's boys help you?"

"No. N-O! No, they didn't help."

"Did you even see them?"

"More than I wanted to."

"What about the big mean one that flipped the June bug down Mrs. Crenshaw's dress? Did you see him?" Opal's eyes were big.

Maggie nodded. "Yep, I saw him. I saw them both, a lot."

"What're their names?"

"The oldest one is Cecil, and the other one is Elbert."

"Is Cecil a troublemaker?" Opal narrowed her eyes.

"Yep."

"Was he mean to you?" Opal pressed.

"Yes."

"What did he do?"

Maggie sighed. "What didn't he do? That is what you should ask." She spread her arms to the sky. "He hit me with a beanie shooter." She rubbed the spot on her cheek. "They strung a rope across the stairs to trip me."

Ruby gasped. "Did you fall?"

"Down the last step! And I slid on my belly across the floor."

"Are you okay?"

Maggie nodded.

"Did they get into trouble?" Opal asked with a delighted gleam in her eye.

"No. I don't know if they ever get into trouble." Maggie shook her head.

"That stinks!" Opal kicked at the dry grass.

"Yes, it does," Maggie agreed.

"What else did they do?" Ruby chimed in.

Maggie took a deep breath. "They accused me of trying to steal Mrs. Crenshaw's salt and pepper shakers and taking Elbert's shirt."

Opal crossed her arms. "I wouldn't go back. Are you?"

Maggie took Opal by the shoulders and looked at her. "Yes, I am going back. If I don't, Daddy has to go to the salt mines.

I have to go back. You have to promise not to tell your mama or my daddy how horrible those boys are." She looked at Ruby. "You have to promise, too!"

"I promise. I don't want our new daddy to leave again." Ruby panicked.

"I promise, too." Opal held up her hand. "I'll swear on a stack of Bibles, and I'll eat grasshoppers. I won't say a word."

"You're not 'spose to swear!" Ruby frowned.

Opal rolled her eyes.

Maggie giggled. It was so much better to be with Opal and Ruby than to be with Cecil and Elbert. "Good!"

"What about Mrs. Crenshaw? Was she nice to you?"

Maggie pursed her lips, thinking of a way to answer. "Mrs. Crenshaw is Mrs. Crenshaw. She treats people like they are beneath her—you know, like they're not as good as she thinks she is." She raised her eyes to see Sue standing on the steps. She hoped Sue hadn't heard too much.

"Maggie, how was your day?" Sue asked.

Maggie smiled. "It was fine, but I'm glad to be home." Her eyes softened as she gazed at the boxcar. She remembered the first time she had seen it, and the hopeless feeling that had surged through her body. Home! Maggie did feel like she was home. This boxcar might be little, but it was a much happier place than the Crenshaw house. It was her home, and she was glad.

The Black Shetland

*M*aggie decided to get up before everyone else and sneak out of the house. She did not want Sue to know about Valina's apple pie. If Sue knew the pie was meant to heap coals of kindness, she would also know that something was wrong at the Crenshaw place. Then she would start asking all those questions grown-ups ask, and she would for sure find out that Mrs. Crenshaw was not a nice person to work for. That would put Maggie's job on the line. So Maggie left a note on the breakfast table, telling the family she wanted to get a head start on all the work while the day was still cool, and tiptoed out the door.

She inhaled. The cool air felt good, but it still carried a dusty dryness. She searched the horizon. No wall of dust clouds. Good! She sure wished for rain. Everybody wished for rain, even if it was too late for the crops this year. Next year was coming, and Daddy had said that the ground was so dry it would take a bunch of rain for him even to consider planting a crop next year.

Maggie skipped and danced. She loved this part of the day, when nothing had happened yet and you could only guess that good things were in store. It was almost like living in a dream world. You could imagine anything you wanted to.

She giggled. Just think what she could make Cecil and Elbert do in her thoughts! Think of Mrs. Crenshaw! Maybe she could have her run up and down the stairs a dozen times. Maybe she could have Cecil hit Mrs. Crenshaw with his beanie shooter. Maybe Mrs. Crenshaw would drop, like Goliath had when King David used his slingshot. Mrs. Crenshaw probably wouldn't be kind enough to lie there and let Cecil whack her head off, though. Maggie laughed. That would make her happy.

Maggie arrived at Valina's back porch and knocked on the door. She listened to Valina sway across the floor, talking to herself. She could hear Valina fiddle with the latch.

"That you, Miss Maggie?"

"Yes, ma'am," Maggie answered.

"You are right early. I haven't been out of bed but a wee bit. Someone light a fire under you?" Valina asked.

"Nope, but it feels like God's about to light a fire. We're heaping the coals, you know." Maggie was wide-eyed.

Valina's deep chuckle filled the room. "We sure are, Missy." She went to the sideboard and picked up the apple pie. It was tied in a white dish towel. The four corners of the towel formed a handle so that Maggie could carry the pie with one hand. "I don't suppose you had yourself any breakfast, leaving as early as you did?"

"No. I had to leave before anyone got up, or Sue would have walked with me and I would have had to tell her everything."

"Umm hmm." Valina gave Maggie a look that showed she understood everything. She turned back to the sideboard and cut a thick slice of bread. "Missy, you hold on there for a minute." Valina brought the bread to the table and smeared it with butter. "Now, Missy, I got what I call my secret sweets." She picked up an old spice shaker with rather large holes in the top and shook it over the buttered bread. "You carry this along with you."

Maggie took the bread and sniffed. There was cinnamon and sugar and she didn't know what else. "Thank you, Mrs. Valina." She took an unladylike bite. "Mmm! That's good."

Valina shook her head. "Missy, Missy!"

"I'm headed to heap coals." Maggie took the pie in one hand and the bread in the other. She stepped out the door, crossed the porch and started for the gate in the tree row. When she hit the street, she shoved the last bite of Valina's bread with the yummy cinnamon-sugar stuff on it into her mouth. She waited until she swallowed before she crossed the street.

As her feet touched the carriage drive, she slowed her pace. She could feel her blood chill. "Please, dear God in my heart, be with me today." She had to force her feet to move.

"Cecil! Elbert!" Mrs. Crenshaw called from the front porch. She shaded her eyes with her hand while she searched the grounds for the boys. When she saw Maggie, she stopped. "Maggie!" she yelled. "Go check on the boys. They aren't in their room, and there's no telling what they are up to."

Maggie paused. She still held the pie in her hand, and she didn't know what to do with it.

"Well, go look for them, girl." Mrs. Crenshaw waved her arm.

Maggie took the pie and headed around the side of the house. The boys were probably out with the bull again. It wouldn't be very smart if they were, but then, Cecil and Elbert didn't seem very smart to Maggie. In fact, if they were with that bull, Maggie would just leave them there and watch.

She plodded up to the fence. The brown bull with the black splotches grazed next to the windmill. Only the sleeve of Elbert's red shirt still hung from his horn. Maggie giggled. Every time the bull moved his head, the red shirtsleeve danced. The bull must have gotten used to it, because he wasn't charging after it anymore.

Maggie scanned the pasture. Cecil and Elbert weren't there. She turned to leave and heard the boys.

"I bet I can ride him!"

Maggie rolled her eyes. The voice belonged to Cecil. She guessed she'd better find out what animal he was going to ride. She headed toward the sound.

"He ain't big enough to be mean."

"What if it's a baby horse, and you ain't 'spose to ride it?" asked Elbert.

"Ah, it ain't no baby. It's just little, but it's a lot bigger than me." Cecil grinned.

Maggie walked around the barn and to the corral. "Cecil, did you ask your aunt if you could ride that horse?" she asked.

"That ain't none of your business." He climbed the fence.

"Cecil, I don't think it's a good idea. What if the horse throws you?" Maggie hoped to scare him into not riding.

"He's a little horse. He ain't going to throw me."

"First of all, the horse is not a he. It's a she."

"And just how do you know that?" Cecil wagged his head.

Maggie hesitated. There was no way she was going to explain this to Cecil and Elbert. "Just take it from me. That horse is a girl."

Cecil squinted. "It don't matter, anyway. It's a little horse, and I'm going to ride it." He refused to call the horse a she.

"Cecil, it's a little horse because it's a Shetland," Maggie told him.

"So?" Cecil sat on top of the fence and cocked his head to the side.

Maggie spread one hand in the air. "Shetlands have about the worst personality of the whole lot of horses that walk the face of the earth."

Cecil laughed. "Like Aunt Louise?"

Elbert giggled. Maggie didn't say a word out loud, but in her mind she completely agreed.

An evil look flickered in Cecil's eyes. "That Shetland is a girl?"

"Yep." Maggie was relieved. Maybe Cecil would finally believe her.

"Elbert, let's name this crankity old Shetland Louise." With that, he dropped inside the corral, stretched his hand out and walked toward the horse. "Here, Louise!" he called.

The black Shetland laid her ears back and watched Cecil come closer. She never let her eyes leave him. She just stood and chewed her grain.

Maggie recognized the ear movement. "Cecil, that horse isn't happy."

"Louise isn't moving. She ain't trying to run away. She likes me," Cecil said.

Maggie shook her head. She tried to warn him one more time.

"Cecil, why don't you turn around and run back to the fence. That horse is about to let you have it."

Cecil sneered, "You're scared. Just watch this!" He eased up to the Shetland. Still the horse stood there.

Only Maggie seemed to notice that the Shetland rolled her black eyes and widened them until the wild whites showed. Maggie shrugged. There was no use in trying to talk Cecil out of it anymore. She might as well watch and see what was going to happen to him.

Cecil grabbed a handful of mane and slung his leg up and over the little horse's back. The Shetland chewed. "See? You're just a scaredy-cat girl. Elbert, want to climb aboard?"

"You bet!" Elbert dropped from the fence and raced toward the Shetland. The horse sidestepped. Elbert stumbled and hit the ground. Dirt sputtered from his mouth. Slowly he got up, sweeping dust from his stomach, still spitting.

Cecil laughed and reached down to help Elbert back on the horse. Elbert hesitated. "Come on, Elbert. You a scaredy-cat girl?"

Elbert frowned, took Cecil's hand and shinnied onto the horse's back. The Shetland merely stood and chewed.

"Come on, you stupid Louise!" Cecil ordered.

The Shetland didn't move.

"I know what I'll do. I've seen the cowboys do it at the rodeo. They kick their horse, and the horse goes. Ready, Elbert?"

Elbert wrapped his arms around Cecil in a wrestler's lock. Cecil held the Shetland's mane with one hand and raised his other high in the air. "Yee-haw! Let her rip, Louise!" He jabbed both sides of the horse with his heels.

Louise jolted, spun, bucked and stampeded into a dead run.

Cecil's waving arm shot down for another handful of mane. His eyes looked like they were about to jump out of his head. Elbert's eyes slapped shut, and he gritted his teeth.

"Turn, Louise, you stupid horse! You're heading straight for the fence!" Cecil screamed.

Louise continued to head for the fence. Maggie held her breath. There was no way the Shetland could jump the fence. She was too short. Then Maggie saw the water trough and smiled. The Shetland was not going to jump the fence.

Cecil was still screaming. "Louise! Horse! Shetland!"

Elbert bawled. Cecil's hair blew straight back from his head. His legs were spread wide, and his hands clutched the horse's mane. Tears flew off the sides of his face.

Just before she reached the water trough, Louise planted her front feet and dipped her head. Cecil and Elbert shot off the Shetland's back and into the trough.

Splash!

Cecil and Elbert came up gasping. Waves flew as their arms frantically fought the water. The Shetland rolled her lips back and whinnied. Maggie giggled. She thought the whinny must be the horse's laugher. Then the black Shetland reached down, took a mouthful of Cecil's shirt and a little bit of his skin, and yanked.

"Yeow!" Cecil screamed.

Louise pranced about with a mouthful of shirt. Maggie slapped her hand over her mouth. If Cecil was hurt, she didn't want to laugh. If he wasn't hurt, she wanted to bust a gut. It served Cecil right.

"What are you boys doing in the horse trough?" Mrs. Crenshaw braced herself with her hands on her hips. She turned to

Maggie. "Have you no better sense than to let them jump in that filthy, stinking water?"

Maggie swallowed. "I was too late to stop them, ma'am. I tried, but they just wouldn't listen."

Cecil stood in the sludge of the grimy, green, mossy water tank. He watched the Shetland. There was no way he was getting back in the corral with that horse, but in order to climb the fence he would have to turn his back on Louise. He spat. He aimed for the ground, but his teeth were chattering so much that he missed the ground and hit Elbert on the head.

"Hey! Watch what you're doing!" Elbert took a swing at his brother and fell back into the trough. He came up sputtering, wiping the water from his eyes. "I'll get you for this! First you make me ride Louise, then you get me thrown. Then you spit on me!"

Cecil's eyes still followed the Shetland. "Elbert, I didn't make you ride Louise. Remember, it was Maggie's idea."

"What?" Mrs. Crenshaw let her wrath fall on Maggie. "Young lady! I might have known you would try to take advantage of these poor city boys. To think you tried to make them ride a Shetland!" As Mrs. Crenshaw's voice grew louder, its pitch rose.

"I did not. I tried to stop them from riding that mean Shetland. They wouldn't listen to me," Maggie shouted.

"Do not raise your voice to me!" Mrs. Crenshaw reached out and grabbed Maggie's ear. "I will teach you some manners, young lady."

Maggie yanked free. She glared at Cecil. "You'd better tell your aunt the truth."

"You want to make me?" Cecil gloated.

Yes, Maggie wanted to make him. No, not right here in front of Mrs. Crenshaw. She would get a lecture on how to be a lady, and beating up a boy was not being a lady.

"Cecil, you have ruined your shirt." Mrs. Crenshaw shook her finger at him.

"It was her fault." He pointed to Maggie.

Maggie gulped, but before she could say a word, Mrs. Crenshaw spoke. "And that will come out of your wages, too."

"Cecil, you'd better tell the truth. Now!" Maggie threatened.

Cecil and Maggie stared at each other. Cecil was the first to drop his gaze. "Okay. Maggie did tell us not to ride the Shetland, because she said that Shetlands have the meanest, worst disposition of all the animals in the whole world."

"Thank you, Cecil." Maggie turned to Mrs. Crenshaw with relief. She would never have believed Cecil would admit this much to his aunt.

"Yes, that's what she told us, all right," Cecil continued. "Then she told us that the Shetland was a girl, and her name was Louise." He grinned.

Maggie's mouth dropped. She knew she would be in for trouble if Mrs. Crenshaw thought that Maggie had named the Shetland.

Mrs. Crenshaw turned red. Slowly, she pulled up her lower jaw and clenched her teeth. She hissed so quietly that Maggie wasn't sure she heard her right. "Shetlands have the meanest, worst dispositions?"

Maggie watched as a light seemed to switch on in Mrs. Crenshaw's eyes.

"Arnold! Arnold calls that stinking Shetland Louise! Of all the nerve!" Mrs. Crenshaw held her head high, took a deep

breath and gave orders. "Cecil, Elbert, get to the house now! Dry off and change your clothes. Margaret Pearl, there is a stack of dishes waiting for you in the kitchen."

Maggie looked to the two boys. They were as surprised as she was. After Cecil's "Louise" comment, Maggie had expected to lose her job. She felt as though hot coals had fallen down her overalls. Then she remembered the apple pie. She picked it up.

"Wait, Mrs. Crenshaw!" she called. Now was the time to heap coals of kindness. "I brought you a homemade apple pie."

Mrs. Crenshaw stopped and turned toward Maggie. "Why?" She was bewildered.

Maggie shrugged. "So I could be nice to you, I guess."

Mrs. Crenshaw stared. "Nice?"

Maggie nodded. She offered the dish-towel-wrapped pie.

Mrs. Crenshaw didn't have a single word to say. She simply took the pie and walked to the house.

Maggie wished that Cecil didn't have a word to say, either, but he did. "Brown-noser!"

Maggie wanted to shout to the world that she hated Cecil and she didn't like Elbert much better. Instead, she smiled. "I'll bet we have it for lunch. It's a special recipe. We always chop up a couple of onions and put them into our apple pie."

"Ugh!" groaned Elbert.

"That's it! You are trying to poison us all. Just wait until I tell Aunt Louise," Cecil warned.

Maggie grinned. Two could play at this game. She left the boys and went to the kitchen. This time, Mrs. Crenshaw didn't call for her once while she was doing the dishes or say a single word while she fixed dinner. In fact, the silence was uncomfortable. Maggie was glad when Mr. Crenshaw stepped in through the front door.

"Dinner ready?" he asked.

Mrs. Crenshaw left the kitchen and marched into the living room to meet him. Maggie heard her say, "Arnold! First of all, I'll never understand why you took that stupid horse for payment instead of money. You're a banker. You could have foreclosed on those no-good farmers, but no, you had to take their dumb horse. Now, what I want you to explain to me is why you named that no-good, ill-mannered black Shetland Louise!"

Maggie set the pan of cornbread down and quickly covered her mouth with the bottom of her apron. It was Mr. Crenshaw who had named the Shetland Louise? She wanted to hear about this.

CHAPTER 12

Gold and Silver

M aggie could hear Mrs. Crenshaw tap her toe, and in her mind she could see her standing, arms crossed, waiting for Mr. Crenshaw to answer. It wasn't hard to bring her face to mind. Mrs. Crenshaw had used that face on Maggie many times. Her eyes would shoot darts, her mouth would be in a tight, thin, demanding line, and her chin would jut out.

"I'm waiting, Arnold." Mrs. Crenshaw must be nose to nose with her husband by now. "I want to know why you named that blasted Shetland after me."

Mr. Crenshaw stuttered, "Well, it was because..."

Maggie could tell he was in trouble, and it sounded like it was going to be big trouble. She felt sorry for Mr. Crenshaw. He had been nice to her when Mrs. Crenshaw wasn't. At least, Maggie got to go home at night. Mr. Crenshaw couldn't. He lived here with that woman.

"Yes, Arnold?" Mrs. Crenshaw growled. "I'm waiting."

Her toe was still tapping, like seconds ticking away on a clock. Maggie had to do something for Mr. Crenshaw. She looked around the kitchen. Her eyes landed on the pie. Quickly, she grabbed the pie and burst into the living room.

"Mr. Crenshaw, look! I brought an apple pie."

Mr. Crenshaw was flustered but relieved at the interruption.

Mrs. Crenshaw wasn't. "Margaret Pearl! This is a private conversation between Mr. Crenshaw and me concerning that blasted horse."

"You mean that *beautiful* Shetland?" Maggie emphasized the word and tipped her head toward Mrs. Crenshaw, so that Mr. Crenshaw might relate the *beautiful* Shetland with his *beautiful* wife.

An ever-so-slight smile touched his lips. "Maggie, thank you for . . . ah . . . the apple pie."

"Yes, sir." Maggie's face lit up. Mr. Crenshaw had understood.

"Margaret Pearl, get back to the kitchen and make sure the table is ready." Mrs. Crenshaw turned to Mr. Crenshaw. "The horse?"

Maggie peeked around the corner. Mr. Crenshaw gently took Mrs. Crenshaw's shoulders and smiled into her eyes. "I only named the Shetland Louise because she is the most beautiful horse I have ever seen. I named her after the most beautiful woman I have ever known—Louise!"

"Hmm. I wonder..." She let it hang.

"How could you wonder about that, my dear? You are so beautiful."

"And the Shetland's personality had nothing to do with it?" Mrs. Crenshaw squinted. To Maggie, it looked like she was trying to drill holes into his brain.

Mr. Crenshaw shrugged. "I named the horse before I ever knew her personality, so it had to be for her good looks."

Mrs. Crenshaw seemed unable to decide whether to believe him or not. Finally, she gave in. "Okay. You're off the hook—this time." She went to the door and called, "Cecil! Elbert!"

Mr. Crenshaw walked to the kitchen, winked at Maggie and mouthed the words, "Thank you."

Maggie glowed. She wondered how these two had gotten married. They were so different! Then she wondered how they had stayed married. They weren't a bit like Daddy and Sue. When Daddy and Sue were together, they were happy, and she had never heard them talk to each other as Mr. and Mrs. Crenshaw did.

Maggie put her hand over her heart and looked up to the ceiling. "Thank you," she whispered. "Thank you for not letting Daddy marry someone like Mrs. Crenshaw."

Once again, everyone sat at the table except Maggie. Today, she didn't feel as bad as she had yesterday. She knew that Mrs. Crenshaw liked to feel important. Maggie, being a maid, helped her to feel that way.

"Maggie, we are ready for that apple pie." Mrs. Crenshaw didn't even look at her.

"Yes, ma'am." Maggie dished up the pie. She served an extra-big piece to Mr. Crenshaw and was rewarded with a sparkling smile. Mrs. Crenshaw didn't even say thank you.

Cecil and Elbert studied their pieces of pie. Elbert was the first to push his away without touching it. "I'm not hungry."

"Nonsense! Eat your pie," Mrs. Crenshaw told him.

"I'm really not hungry," Elbert lied.

Mrs. Crenshaw put her fork down, "Every ten minutes, you boys beg for something to eat. Don't tell me that you are not hungry. Eat the pie!"

Elbert turned to Cecil. Cecil shrugged his shoulders.

Mrs. Crenshaw crossed her arms on the edge of the table. "Cecil, why aren't you eating your pie?"

Cecil bit his bottom lip.

"I'm waiting." Mrs. Crenshaw watched both of them.

"Louise, if they aren't hungry, don't make them eat the pie," Mr. Crenshaw said. "Besides, I would gladly eat one of their pieces." He dabbed his mouth with his napkin. "That was about the best apple pie I have ever eaten!"

Mrs. Crenshaw glared at him. "You don't need another piece, Arnold. Next time, Maggie, give him a smaller piece."

"Yes, ma'am." Maggie knew she had to answer Mrs. Crenshaw, but she looked at Mr. Crenshaw to see if he forgave her.

He winked.

Mrs. Crenshaw sat back and studied the boys. "Now, tell me. What is the real reason you won't touch that pie?"

Elbert glared at Maggie. "Onions!"

"What on earth do onions have to do with apple pie?"

"Maggie said she put onions in the pie," Elbert wailed.

"Poisoned it, that's what she did," Cecil accused.

"That is nonsense." Mrs. Crenshaw furrowed her brows and searched the remainder of her pie to see if there were any onions in it.

"It ain't nonsense. Maggie told us about the onions," Elbert insisted.

"That pie is poison for sure," Cecil blurted out. "And I ain't eating it!"

Mr. Crenshaw slammed the table with his hand and hee-hawed. "Good idea, Maggie! That means more pie for me."

"You ain't afraid of onions?" Cecil asked.

"Not a bit. In fact, I think they made the pie better. Slide your piece this way."

Cecil shoved his plate to Mr. Crenshaw.

"Arnold!" Everyone could feel the warning in Mrs. Crenshaw's voice, but Mr. Crenshaw ignored it. He loaded his fork with a huge bite and motioned for Maggie.

She walked to his place at the head of the table. "Yes, sir?"

Mr. Crenshaw dug deep into his pocket and pulled out a quarter. "Here you go, Maggie. Thank you for the pie."

"Wow! Yes, sir." Maggie felt the cold silver in her hand. She thought she was rich.

"Arnold! Just what do you think you're doing?" Mrs. Crenshaw's eyebrows arched halfway up her forehead.

Mr. Crenshaw blinked. "You said she was hired help. I gave her a tip."

"We do not tip our hired help."

"I do. In fact, Maggie, thank you for telling the boys that there were onions in the pie. What a wonderful idea!" He reached in his pocket again and dropped another quarter into her hand.

Maggie beamed. She didn't think she had ever held this much money in her whole life.

"Arnold!" Mrs. Crenshaw was livid.

"Louise?" Mr. Crenshaw stared into her eyes, and as if he could read her thoughts, he added, "This tip will not come out of her wages."

Mrs. Crenshaw was ready to explode. Instead, she gained control of herself and shrugged her shoulders. "She hardly has any wages left, anyway."

"Why is that, Louise?" Mr. Crenshaw held his loaded fork poised in mid-air.

"Arnold," she smiled, "I put her in charge of the boys, and she has let each of them ruin a shirt since she has been here. I will deduct the expense of those shirts from her wages. That will not leave her very much."

"Each of the boys?" he asked.

Mrs. Crenshaw nodded.

Mr. Crenshaw turned to Cecil. "What happened to your shirt?"

Cecil swallowed. "That Shetland, Louise, bit a hunk out of my shirt."

"Louise? Hmm. What were you doing so close to the horse?"

"Riding her, sir."

"Really? Did Maggie tell you it was okay to ride the Shetland?"

Cecil and Maggie looked at each other. Cecil dropped his eyes. "She told us not to."

"Then would you say that your torn shirt was her fault?" Mr. Crenshaw asked.

Cecil bit his bottom lip. "No, sir."

"Good. I don't think it was her fault, either." Mr. Crenshaw turned to Elbert. "Now, Elbert, how did Maggie ruin your shirt?"

Elbert flashed a glance at Mrs. Crenshaw before he began. "Cecil was going to make the bull chase him, like they do in rodeos. I was going to help him, only when I saw that the bull was going to kill us, I ran to the fence and dove over. My shirt got stuck on the fence, and I shucked it, fast. Then Maggie grabbed it because it was red, and she went tearing out to save Cecil. She shot between that mad killer bull and Cecil, waving my red shirt."

Cecil made a noise as if to interrupt, but Elbert plowed on. "Then the bull took out after Maggie. I thought she was a goner, but she made it to the windmill. She dove under it and then climbed it. That killer bull kept ramming into the windmill. I thought Maggie was going to die. Finally, she dropped the shirt on the killer bull's head, and it caught on his horn. He went wild across the pasture. I think my shirt is still hooked on his horn, if you want to see it."

Mr. Crenshaw raised his eyebrows. "I may take a look later. It sounds like you three had quite an exciting day. It also sounds like Maggie may have saved your life, Cecil." He turned to Mrs. Crenshaw. "Louise, do you really think she needs to pay for Elbert's shirt?"

"Someone has to. Maggie was in charge of the boys."

Mr. Crenshaw sighed. "Maggie, did you or did you not tell the boys they could play rodeo with the bull?"

Mrs. Crenshaw interrupted. "You know what her answer will be. She will deny it."

"Louise! Very well. Elbert, did Maggie tell you to play rodeo with the bull?" Mr. Crenshaw was serious.

"Heck, no! She told us to stay out of there, but Cecil called her a scaredy-cat."

"Thank you, Elbert. And no more of that language."

"Yes, sir."

"Well, Louise, I think it is pretty clear. The shirts will not come out of Maggie's wages."

"But…"

"That is final, Louise."

Maggie could tell that Mrs. Crenshaw didn't like this a bit. She knew she'd probably be in for it this afternoon.

Mr. Crenshaw watched his wife's smoldering silence, then turned to Maggie. "Maggie, I want you to make it an early day today. After the dishes, you go ahead and go home."

Mrs. Crenshaw gasped.

"On second thought, today Cecil and Elbert will do the dishes. That should help pay for their shirts. Maggie, I'll walk you down the carriage drive. We will chat."

Cecil groaned. Elbert dropped his head to the table.

"Maggie, shall we?" Mr. Crenshaw stood up and offered her his hand.

Maggie swallowed. "Are you sure it's okay?"

"It's my house. It will be fine."

When they stepped out of the kitchen, Maggie glimpsed back and saw Mrs. Crenshaw pick up a bowl and throw it across the room. It crashed at Cecil's feet. "Eeyow!" he yelled.

"Pick it up!" Mrs. Crenshaw ordered. "Every last piece of it!"

Maggie wondered if this was the effect of the hot coals. She looked up at Mr. Crenshaw to see if he had heard what happened in the kitchen. She watched a smile flicker over him, but he didn't flinch or say a word.

With her hand in Mr. Crenshaw's big hand, Maggie's heart soared. She stuck her free hand deep into her pocket and felt the two quarters. Wow! The God in her heart was good.

CHAPTER 13

"Mama"

A t the gate in the tree row, Mr. Crenshaw stopped and knelt on one knee to face her. "Maggie, on payday you come and see me. I will pay you at dinnertime. That way, we won't have to bother Mrs. Crenshaw. She has enough on her mind."

"Thank you, sir." Maggie smiled. He made her feel safe, and she really thought he liked her. She didn't think Mrs. Crenshaw did. Maggie wasn't sure that Mrs. Crenshaw liked anyone.

Mr. Crenshaw swung the gate open for her. "Are you sure you can make it home by yourself from here?"

"Yes, sir. I did yesterday."

"Okay, young lady. I'll see you tomorrow." He closed the gate after Maggie and waved.

When he was out of sight, she grabbed the quarters, kissed them and twirled. "Valina! Valina!" She ran to Valina's house.

Valina met her at the door. "Gracious, Missy, what be the matter?"

"The matter? Not a thing! Our heaping coals of kindness is working."

"Well, the good Lord said it would. Come tell me all about it."

Maggie sat down and plopped the two quarters on top of the kitchen table.

"You get paid today?" Valina asked.

"Not wages. This is tip money. Part of it is yours. For the pie!" Maggie's eyes sparkled.

"Tip money?"

"Yep. Mr. Crenshaw gave me tip money for bringing the pie, and tip money for telling Cecil and Elbert it had onions in it."

"Why?"

"Because then Mr. Crenshaw could eat their pieces of pie, too," Maggie giggled.

"I'm sure he liked that, Missy, but why did you tell Cecil and Elbert there were onions in the pie?" Valina sat across from Maggie.

"Oh," Maggie sighed, "I guess I let my temper get a hold of me. Those boys make me so mad! They had just blamed me for naming that black Shetland Louise. That's Mrs. Crenshaw's name, you know."

"Mmm!" Valina shook her head.

Maggie leaned across the table. "Do you know who did name the Shetland? It was Mr. Crenshaw. Can you believe that?"

"Lord have mercy! Mr. Crenshaw must be a braver soul than I thought."

"He is. He let me leave early, and he made Cecil and Elbert pay for their own shirts by doing the dishes."

"Wait a minute, Missy. You got some explaining to do. I'll fetch a couple of glasses of tea and you fill me in on everything." Valina gathered two glasses and a pitcher of tea. While she poured, Maggie poured out the rest of the story. Valina's rich laughter added to the joy of the day's events.

Maggie ended with, "You know, Mrs. Valina, I feel kind of sorry for Mrs. Crenshaw. She doesn't seem to like Cecil and Elbert very much, and I think she hates me. I'm sure glad my daddy didn't marry someone like that."

"Mmm, Missy, you be a lucky child. Mrs. Sue has a heart big enough to love a load of children." Valina smiled.

"Mrs. Valina?"

"Yes, Missy."

Maggie silently traced beads of water down her glass.

"Something bothering you, Missy?"

Maggie felt a cold surge through her. She badly wanted to ask Valina a question, but she didn't know whether she wanted to show her heart.

"Missy, you done swore me to secrecy, so I guess you can ask me just about anything you want to." Valina reached across the table and covered Maggie's wet hand with her warm one.

Maggie felt the warmth spread through her, giving her courage. "Mrs. Valina, Sue told me I could call her Mama."

"If she told you that, she means it with her whole heart. That lady has the love of God flowing through her veins. If you're asking me, 'Does she really mean it?' I'd say I'd stake my life on it." Valina patted Maggie's hand.

Maggie lifted her eyes to Valina. Silent tears trickled down her cheeks. She shook her head. "I know Sue means it. She really does love me, and I love her." Silence followed.

Valina whispered, "Then what's the matter, Missy?"

"Valina, if I call Sue Mama, does it mean I don't love my mama anymore? Can my mama in heaven hear me call Sue

Mama on earth? Will it hurt my mama's feelings?" Maggie sobbed.

"You come here, child." Valina went to her rocker and pulled Maggie onto her lap. "Missy, I don't know all there is to know about heaven, but I'm going to tell you what I know about being a mama." She wiped Maggie's eyes with the hem of her apron. "Missy, my three girls are in heaven. If they need to crawl up on your mama's lap while I'm not there for them, it will be fine by me. If they need to call your mama 'Mama,' I would be honored if your mama would let them."

"Then you think it is okay with my mama if I call Sue Mama?"

"Yes, Miss Maggie. I surely do."

For a long time, Maggie and Valina cried and rocked together.

CHAPTER 14

Tip Money

Maggie determined that the first thing she would do when she got home would be to call Sue Mama. It would feel so good to say "Mama" again!

She reached deep into her pocket and clicked the quarters together. She still had the two, because Valina had refused to take one for her apple pie. She hadn't thought it was right to take money for the fuel to heap coals of kindness. Maggie couldn't wait to show the quarters to Opal and Ruby. They would be so surprised!

With her other hand, Maggie swung the basket she was carrying. Valina had sent her home with goodies. There were two jars of strawberry jam; one was to be the coals of kindness for tomorrow, and the other was for Maggie's family. She smiled as she remembered Valina telling her about the strawberry patch, and how Mr. Gatlin had told her that he didn't really like the strawberries because they were too seedy, so if she wanted to have Martin plow up the patch, that would be fine. Valina had had Martin dig up the strawberries and replant them behind her house. Valina chuckled when she said, "The good Lord can even use people like Mr. Thomas Gatlin."

The basket also held some old flour sacks Mr. Thomas Gatlin was going to throw away. Valina told Maggie she was sure that with three little girls to dress, Sue could use them. Maggie peeked at the sacks. They had little circles of dainty blue flowers. She was glad Valina hadn't thrown them away, for she knew Sue would use them.

The dry grass crunched as Maggie crossed the pasture. She watched Lulubelle, who stood beneath the big cottonwood swishing flies with her tail. Maggie heard Opal and Ruby before she saw them. She stood still, to try and hear what they were saying and see where they were.

"You think Lulubelle will mind?" Ruby asked.

"She's a cow. How could a cow mind?" Opal replied.

Maggie held her hand over her eyes and searched the area around Lulubelle. They must be close to the cow, since they were talking about her.

"If Lulubelle stands real still, I think I can drop on her. When I get on her back, you follow me."

Maggie's shoulders sank. She felt as though she was with Cecil and Elbert again. "Don't do it!" she yelled, as she ran for the tree.

The voices hushed. A head popped out of the cottonwood. "Maggie? What are you doing here?" Opal asked.

Maggie ignored the question. "What are you doing up there?"

"We were just going to sit on Lulubelle's back."

"Opal was. I didn't want to." Ruby glared at Opal.

"Hey, Maggie, have you seen that cute little horse that the Crenshaws have?" Opal wanted to know.

Maggie laughed. "Yep. I met that horse today. She is a Shetland, and she may be cute and she may be little, but I'd rather ride a wild buffalo. You'll have to ask Cecil and Elbert about riding that cute little horse."

"I won't ask those two nothing. Not after the way they treated me on Sunday." Opal jutted her bottom lip.

"You should. It would be really funny to see the look on their faces." Maggie beamed.

"What happened?" Opal dropped from the tree and held out her hands to catch Ruby.

"The Shetland dumped them both into the horse tank. Then she bit a hunk out of Cecil's shirt."

"I wish I could have seen that," Opal giggled.

"You would have died laughing." Maggie chuckled as she remembered. "You taking Lulubelle in to milk?"

Opal nodded.

"Opal wanted to ride her." Ruby looked up at Maggie. "I told her it wasn't a good idea, but she told me I was just a kid and wouldn't know a good thing if it looked me in the eye."

Maggie laughed. "Opal, you might listen to Ruby, even if she is a kid. It will keep you out of trouble."

"I just wanted to save a few steps. Plus, I thought it would be fun," Opal reasoned.

"Listen, there is a reason we ride horses and not cows. Cows don't like it," Maggie explained.

"Why?"

"Ask God," Maggie told her, because she didn't know the answer. She just knew that people didn't ride cows except at rodeos, and then they got bucked off.

"We could try it. Lulubelle likes us. I could ride, and you

could guide." Opal was determined to ride the cow.

About that time, a gossipy magpie swooshed across Lulu-belle's back. Lulubelle bawled and bucked, kicking tufts of dry grass over their heads. Maggie threw Ruby behind her. Opal stumbled backwards and fell smack on her backside.

Maggie doubled over with laughter. "Do you still want to ride Lulubelle?"

Opal dusted herself and shook her head.

"Girls!" Sue ran toward them. "Are you all right?"

Ruby plunged into the safety of Sue's arms. "Maggie saved my life! She pulled me away from Lulubelle's feet." Ruby's eyes were huge.

"Maggie, thank you." Sue stroked Ruby's hair.

"She saved Opal's life, too," Ruby continued.

"She did? How?"

"Maggie wouldn't let Opal ride Lulubelle. She told her that we ride horses, not cows. But Opal wanted to do it anyway."

"Blabbermouth!" Opal stood with her hands on her hips.

"Opal is just lazy. That's why she wanted to ride Lulubelle," Ruby said.

"Tattletale!"

"Opal, I don't ever want you trying to ride Lulubelle. I know she seems like a nice, gentle cow, but she scares very easily. You could get hurt, or even killed. I want you to promise you won't try that again." Sue had no smile as she warned Opal.

Opal glared at Ruby, but she gave her word.

"Now, both of you tell Maggie 'thank you.'"

Ruby hugged Maggie, making sure the cow was on the other side, but Opal only kicked at the ground and mumbled, "Thanks."

Sue turned to Maggie. "What we would do without you is a mystery. I thank God for you every day."

"Thank you," Maggie whispered, then swallowed. This was it. This was the time when she could call Sue Mama. Her heart wanted to, but "Sue" was the word that tumbled out of her lips. A small silence followed. Maggie's heart dropped as she looked into Sue's eyes and saw the hurt they held. Maggie wanted to fix it, but she didn't know how.

"Well, we'd better get Lulubelle in to milk." Sue turned to the cow.

Maggie thought Sue had turned away because she was going to cry and she didn't want the girls to see her. Maggie had to do something. She looked around, trying to think. Her eyes lit on the basket. "Hey! I brought a surprise from Valina." She swung the basket in a circle.

The girls rushed for the basket. Sue watched them and smiled, but she stayed by the cow with her hand on the lead rope.

Ruby danced. Opal grabbed.

Maggie shook her head. "Not until supper." She liked the suspense.

As they headed for the lean-to, Maggie heard pounding. She looked up. Daddy was on top of the boxcar, fixing the roof. Wow! He really was feeling better. Her heart skipped a beat. Was he better enough to go back to work? Would her job be enough to keep him here? She thought of the quarters in her pocket. Her heart surged. That would be the best surprise at supper. Surely it would keep him at home.

The girls rushed through their chores, tumbled into the house, washed up and piled onto the bench at the table. As soon as the "amen" ended the prayer, their questions began.

"What's in the basket?"

"Is it for all of us?"

"Is it something we can eat?"

"Is it alive?"

Daddy laughed. "If it's alive, don't open the basket until I've eaten. I'm not wanting to share my supper. Nothing is going to take my biscuits and gravy away from me."

"A puppy!" Ruby clapped.

"No, Ruby, I can tell it's not a puppy. Puppies make too much noise." Opal took a biscuit and tossed one on Ruby's plate.

"You don't know. It could be a puppy, and he might be asleep." Ruby glared.

Maggie interrupted, "Don't eat the biscuits!"

Daddy already had a bite of one of the biscuits jammed in his mouth. Sue had just picked one off the plate.

Maggie opened the basket and set the jar of strawberry jam in the middle of the table. "Wow!" Ruby's face shone.

"Yippy!" Opal shouted.

"Strawberry?" Sue asked.

"Hand me another biscuit," Daddy mumbled around his mouthful.

Everyone laughed. Maggie couldn't help but think of the difference between meals here and at the Crenshaws'. She loved mealtimes here, even if they were simple. There might be more to eat at the Crenshaws', but something was missing. Whatever it was, Maggie wouldn't trade meals at her home for theirs. Not in a million years!

"We will have to thank Valina." Sue's voice was soft.

"There's more!" Maggie beamed. She pulled out the flour sacks. "Valina got these from Mr. Thomas Gatlin. He was going to throw them away. She knew you could use them."

Sue gasped. "This is what I've been praying for. Material! Now I can make you a dress to work in, Maggie." Her eyes glistened with the promise of tears.

Daddy laid his fork down and put his arm about Sue. "God is good."

"And that isn't all." Maggie was so excited that she hadn't touched her food. She dug into her pocket, drug out the two quarters and clanked them on the table in front of her daddy's plate.

Opal and Ruby sucked in their breath. Sue raised her eyebrows.

"Payday?" Daddy asked.

"Tip day!" Maggie giggled. "Payday is still coming."

Opal was amazed. "You must be a really good worker to get tips."

"A tip from Mrs. Crenshaw?" Sue searched Maggie's eyes.

Maggie shook her head. "Not Mrs. Crenshaw, Mr. Crenshaw. And Mrs. Crenshaw didn't like it."

"I'll just bet she didn't," Sue said quietly, as she slid a knowing look toward Daddy.

"I'm proud of you, Maggie." Daddy patted her hand.

"Now you won't have to go to the salt mines." Maggie was so excited that she could feel her heart pound in her ears.

Silence settled around the table. Daddy looked at Sue. Sue shook her head so slightly that Maggie wasn't sure it had really happened. All of a sudden, she wasn't hungry. "Daddy, you aren't going back there, are you?"

Daddy dropped his eyes and kept silent. Maggie could tell he didn't know what to say.

Sue answered, "Maggie, your daddy doesn't feel right taking your money."

"He isn't taking it. I'm giving it!" Maggie jumped and leaned over the edge of the table. "I prayed to the God in my heart. He gave me this job so Daddy wouldn't have to go away again."

No one spoke a word.

Maggie searched their faces. "Daddy, you can't go away. You can't go!" Tears stormed down her cheeks. Still Daddy didn't answer, and in the silence Maggie knew that he was going. She didn't know when, but she knew he was going.

Maggie slid from the bench, flew out the door, stumbled down the steps and into the dusky evening. The slam of the screen door echoed through the darkening night.

A Handful of Stars

The cool night breeze brushed through the lone cottonwood, making the moon-soaked leaves dance. Their waltz was accompanied by a gentle tinkling as the leaves twirled and touched each other. Maggie thought she could stay here forever. In the tree, she felt hidden from the rest of the world. That was exactly what she wanted right now.

Maggie lay back on a thick cottonwood branch and let its slow sway rock the tears away. Mr. Thomas Gatlin! He was the reason Daddy would have to go away, and yet he was the reason they'd had strawberry jam for supper tonight. He didn't know he'd had a part in their supper, but Maggie would have liked for him to know it. She would like to see the startled expression on his face if she could tell him, "Thank you for the strawberry jam. My daddy, especially, loved it." A wicked smile slid into place. That's what she would like to do, but that is not what she would do.

Maggie looked up at the moon through the cottonwood leaves. Somewhere up there was heaven. Mama was there.

Daddy would be in Hutchinson before long. Hutchinson ... heaven. For Maggie, one was just as far away as the other. She wouldn't be able to see him or touch him or talk to him. The empty hole in her heart got deeper and bigger. She wondered how long it would be before it swallowed her whole being.

"Maggie! I know you're up there."

It was Daddy. Maggie shivered in silence.

"Maggie, I can climb trees, too."

Maggie knew she should answer, but she didn't.

"Okay." Daddy swung up into the tree.

Maggie wondered if Daddy could hear the pounding of her heart. She knew she should say something, but it was a little late now.

"Maggie." Daddy crawled on a branch beside her. "Maggie."

Maggie bit her bottom lip and tried to watch the stars. The waxy leaves chattered. Maggie thought they were the only ones that knew what to say. She didn't, and it seemed like Daddy didn't, either.

"This tree is a fine tree," Daddy said. "Your mama would have liked it."

"Mama liked trees?"

"Especially cottonwoods. She's the one who planted the little cottonwood in front of the house." He paused. "Maggie, you remind me a lot of your mama."

"How?"

"In almost every way. You walk like her. Your eyes sparkle when you laugh, like hers did. You even giggle the same. Sometimes I hear her in your voice." He slowed to a stop.

"Daddy, I miss her."

Daddy swallowed. "I do, too." He broke a leaf from the branch and toyed with it. "Mama is like this leaf. It is still beautiful, but it is not a part of the tree anymore. Maggie, your mama is still beautiful, even if she is not with us."

"I wish I could talk to her."

"What would you say?"

"I don't know. I think when she was here I didn't say the important things. I wish I could tell her I love her, and I wish I could ask her things, and I wish..." Maggie broke off a twig and threw it through the leaves. "Mama's up there in the stars, but it is so far away! I can't touch her. I might as well try to hold a star."

"Maggie, you're holding a star right now."

"What?"

"There is a star in your hand."

"Daddy, there's a stick in my hand."

Maggie could feel Daddy smile. "Cottonwood stick. Look at the end of the stick you just broke off."

Maggie turned the stick toward the moonlight so she could see the tip.

"Do you see the star?"

"Oh, yes!" Maggie gasped. "There is a star!"

"Hmm," Daddy nodded. "There is always a star when you break a cottonwood stick. See, Maggie, you are holding a star in your hand. Those stars are not so far away as you thought. Neither is your mama."

"But she feels far away." The yearning twisted within Maggie. "Sometimes I just want to talk to her."

"Maggie, you have a personal messenger who can. You can ask God to tell her anything you want."

"And He will do it?"

Daddy shrugged. "He's a God of miracles, isn't He?"

Maggie broke her stick into tiny pieces. She needed a miracle now. It would take one to keep her daddy with her. "Daddy, when are you going?"

"In a week. Dr. Nelson says I'll be ready then."

"Couldn't you wait and see if Mrs. Crenshaw pays me enough for our family to make ends meet?" Maggie whispered.

"Honey, I wouldn't be much of a man if I lived by hiring out my little girl."

"But I don't mind. I want to! You'd be close." She closed her eyes. "Daddy, Hutchinson is as far away as heaven." She rolled the broken sticks in her hand.

Daddy chuckled. "Not by a long shot! Hutchinson is a whole lot closer than heaven."

Maggie didn't laugh.

"I'll tell you what. I'll spend this week looking for a job right here in Dodge City. How about that?"

"And if you find one?" Maggie asked. Now she had hope—a whole week of hope. A whole week for the God in her heart to work His miracle.

"If I find one, I'll stay."

"Yippy!" Maggie giggled.

Daddy was silent. A soft breeze played with the leaves. "But Maggie, if I don't find one, I will go," he warned. "I will have to leave you with Sue and the girls. Sue is a good lady, and I believe she loves you. I know she will take care of you, and she can teach you the lady things you need to know. Maggie, don't be afraid of her." Daddy reached over to cover Maggie's hand with his.

"Afraid of Sue? I'm not. Sue is nice, and I'm glad you married her." Maggie wanted to add that she was glad he hadn't married someone like Mrs. Crenshaw. "It's just that when you are gone, I feel like I've lost you, too."

"You haven't, Maggie. And, the good Lord willing, you won't."

"Well, I'm going to ask the God in heaven and the God in my heart to keep you here." Maggie stated it as a fact and a done deal.

"You talk to Him about it, Maggie." Daddy sighed and stretched his stiff legs. "As much as I like this cottonwood, I think we'd better get you to bed. Morning comes early, and you're a working girl."

Maggie giggled again. Daddy lowered himself down a couple of branches and jumped to the ground. He held his arms up to catch Maggie. When she tumbled into them, he didn't set her down. He held his little girl.

Maggie locked her arms around his neck. "I love you, Daddy!"

"I love you, Margaret Pearl," he whispered into her dishwater-blond hair.

Maggie smiled. Daddy had used the names both her mamas had given her, and it felt good.

Daddy carried her to the front steps of the boxcar house and gently placed her on the top step. Softly, he kissed her cheek. Maggie stood on the step, searching her daddy's eyes. Her own began to sparkle. In the shower of moonlight, she shoved her tight fist in front of Daddy.

"Guess what I've got?" she asked.

"What, Pumpkin?"

"Guess!"

"Wishes?"

She giggled. "Sort of." Maggie unfolded her hand. Tiny pieces of broken cottonwood twigs lay scattered over her palm. "A whole handful of stars!"

CHAPTER 16

Payday

Maggie twirled, spreading her new dress like an umbrella. It was beautiful. Sue had finished it last night. She had cut the bottom off Maggie's oldest, raggiest pair of overalls, saying, "Those legs are so thin I can see through them. I don't know how many times the knees have been patched!" She then gathered the flour sacks into a skirt and sewed them to the bib of the overalls.

Maggie loved her new dress. Mrs. Crenshaw had given her a week to work in "boy's clothes." When Maggie had told her that she couldn't come up with a dress by the end of the first week, Mrs. Crenshaw had extended the deadline to three weeks. But Maggie had been wrong. Her week wasn't up until the end of today, and here she was, decked out in a new dress. The God in her heart sure was good! Maggie twirled again. She had a new dress, and this was payday. This had to be one of the best days of her life.

The only drawback was Daddy. The week he had promised her was half gone, and still there was no job. Thinking about it made Maggie's heart pound a little faster. She squeezed her

eyes tight. "Dear God in my heart, you've just got to help my daddy find a job in the next few days. I don't know how I can get along without him. And, God, now there are Sue and Opal and Ruby, too. They love him as much as I do. Please, can you keep him here for us all?"

Maggie looked up at the sky. A warm smile spread across her face. It still amazed her that God way out there could hear her prayers from way down here. How it worked, she didn't know, but it did work. She had a new dress to prove it.

"Morning to you!" Valina waved from her back porch.

Maggie twirled to show off her new dress.

"Well, look at you! Don't you look mighty fancy?" Valina chuckled.

"Sue finished it last night from those flower sacks you sent home a few days ago. I think Sue can do anything." Maggie glowed.

Valina paused for a moment. "Yes, Miss Maggie, I think that new mama of yours can do anything."

Maggie dropped her eyes. "Valina, it just doesn't feel right. I know she's one of the best things that has happened to Daddy and me since Mama died, but when I try to make myself call her Mama it won't work. I know I am terrible and ungrateful." She could feel the tears exploding.

"Now, child!" Valina wrapped her arms around Maggie. "You are not terrible and ungrateful. These matters of the heart take themselves some time. Settle down and take a deep breath."

Maggie inhaled and looked at Valina.

"Mmm. Can you just smell our heaping coals today?" Valina swung open the screen door, and Maggie followed her into the kitchen.

"Donuts!"

Valina beamed. "I had to threaten Martin to keep him from eating them all."

"They make my tummy rumble." Maggie could feel her mouth water, too.

"There's plenty. You can have you one."

Maggie grabbed a donut and took a big bite. She closed her eyes and chewed. "Mmm! Valina, do you think they have these in heaven?"

Valina chuckled. "I reckon they do. My mama taught me to make them, and she's already there. But in heaven they are most likely made with heavenly sugar, so a person won't be adding extra pounds. I'd sure hate to fall through the clouds that hold up those golden streets."

Maggie giggled as she swallowed the last of her donut.

Valina stuffed most of the remaining donuts into Maggie's basket. "You had best drink this glass of milk and be on your way." She slid the glass across the table to Maggie.

Maggie gulped it down, grabbed the basket and headed to the door. "Thanks, Valina. Are you sure you saved enough for Mr. Martin?"

"You don't worry none. I saved him more than he needs. You best get going now, child." Her warm hand patted Maggie's cheek. "You go have you a good day."

"I will. Nothing can go wrong today. It's payday!" Maggie bounced out the door and turned to wave.

Valina was still watching her when she reached the gate. Maggie thought she probably did that every day. Valina had helped her so much! Maybe Maggie could give her some money for all she had done. No, she threw that thought aside. There was no way Valina would take money from her. Maybe she could get her something special. That would work. She would get something special for Valina.

Maggie took a deep breath as she laid her hand on the gate latch. The walk across the pasture in the early morning and her few minutes with Valina were her special time. Once she entered the gate, her time didn't belong to her anymore. Mrs. Crenshaw owned it.

Maggie opened the gate and stepped through. She pretty well had her routine down now: she dropped off her "coals of kindness" in the kitchen, did the morning dishes—which were usually last night's supper dishes and today's breakfast dishes together—and then she checked on the boys. When Mrs. Crenshaw was ready to fix dinner, she hollered for Maggie. Then Maggie helped in the kitchen, served dinner and cleaned up. She especially looked forward to dinner, because she felt that Mr. Crenshaw liked her and was glad to have her there. After she had cleaned up, she would check on the boys. The rest of the afternoons were usually spent with Cecil and Elbert. Thursday had been her worst day—she had ironed all afternoon.

Today was special, she reminded herself. Today was payday. Maggie walked up the lane to the Crenshaws' door and knocked.

"Well, come in, girl," Mrs. Crenshaw told her. She seldom called her Maggie. "It's about time."

"Yes, ma'am." Maggie always answered this way. It seemed to make Mrs. Crenshaw feel better, and besides, Sue had told her to. Maggie took an extra big step to let her new dress swish. She wanted Mrs. Crenshaw to notice.

Mrs. Crenshaw furrowed her forehead and looked Maggie up and down. "I suppose that is a dress."

"Yes, ma'am." Maggie's eyes sparkled.

Mrs. Crenshaw shook her head. If Maggie was hoping for more, she was out of luck. Maggie was glad she had stopped by Valina's this morning. At least Valina had liked her dress.

Maggie took her heaping coals to the sideboard in the kitchen and set the basket down. Mrs. Crenshaw stretched her neck to see what was in the basket today. She would never say a word to Maggie, not even a thank you, but Maggie could tell that she looked forward to the special basket more and more each day.

Cecil and Elbert were a different story. They tumbled into the kitchen with eager smiles. "What did you bring today?" Elbert asked.

Cecil jabbed him. "She ain't going to tell you until she's good and ready."

"It smells good. I want to know!" Elbert rubbed his tummy.

"Tell the boys and put them out of their misery," Mrs. Crenshaw ordered.

Maggie thought it might put Mrs. Crenshaw out of her misery, too. "All right, I'll show you. But it is a look and not a touch." She swept the dish towel off the basket.

Cecil's eyes popped wide. Elbert wrapped his arms around his stomach and groaned, "I'm dying!"

"Please, Maggie!" Cecil begged.

"Not until dinner." Maggie pulled the basket away.

"We'll do a chore for you," Elbert promised.

Maggie thought about that. She had plenty of chores. "My pick?"

Elbert shrugged. "Okay."

"Cecil?" Maggie waited for an answer.

"As long as it ain't no big chore, like the dishes," he challenged.

Maggie thought for a moment. "No big chore." She agreed and held out her hand.

Cecil was still hesitant. Elbert wasn't. He latched onto her hand and gave it a quick, hearty shake. Maggie thought he was almost drooling.

Slowly, Cecil held out his hand. "You got yourself a deal."

Maggie grabbed his hand to seal the bargain. "Deal."

Elbert reached for the basket, but Maggie yanked it away again. "First you do the chore. Then you get the payment."

"That so, Cecil?" Elbert asked.

Cecil turned to Mrs. Crenshaw. "Is it, Aunt Louise?"

Mrs. Crenshaw blinked. Maggie could tell that she hated to agree, but she nodded.

"Okay, what's the chore?" Elbert was ready to get it over with. The donuts were all he could think about.

"Empty the slop buckets." Maggie smiled.

"You're out of your head if you think I'm touching slop buckets," Cecil roared.

A doomed look crossed Elbert's face. "That ain't fair!"

Maggie shrugged. "We shook. It's too late to back out now. It's the chore for the donuts."

Cecil glared. "Then I don't want no donut!"

Elbert swallowed. He seemed to turn green as Maggie watched. "I do. Can't you give us something else?"

"That's the deal, Elbert, and a real man sticks to anything he shakes hands on." Maggie crossed her arms.

"You don't know nothing about real men!" Cecil stormed. "Besides, Elbert and I are just kids, so we don't have to stick to our word. Right, Aunt Louise?"

"How do you think you learn to stick to your word if you don't start when you're a kid?" Maggie took a step toward him and glared into his eyes.

Cecil backed away. "Aunt Louise?"

Mrs. Crenshaw took a deep breath and let it out slowly. Maggie thought she must be trying to find a way to tell them yes, they did have to keep their word, yet still make it so the boys wouldn't have to do Maggie's chore. Finally, she spoke.

"Cecil, Elbert, you will have to keep your word. It is what all God's people should do. However, there is a lesson to be learned here. Beware of charlatans who will make you give your word before you know what you are giving your word on."

"We have to empty the slop buckets?" Cecil wailed.

Mrs. Crenshaw nodded. The boys hung their heads and slunk from the kitchen.

Mrs. Crenshaw turned to Maggie. "I am very disappointed in you. You have tricked those two innocent boys into doing the most unpleasant chore you have. Don't think this will be forgotten. You are going to march right behind them and clean up any mess they make. Do you understand me?"

Maggie blinked. "Yes, ma'am." Quickly, she turned and got out of the room. She had started up the stairs when she remembered that she'd forgotten to cover the donuts. There were too many flies around to leave them that way. She ran back to the kitchen, but stopped in the doorway.

Mrs. Crenshaw was shoving a donut into her mouth. Maggie froze. Slowly, she stepped back before Mrs. Crenshaw could see her. Then she turned and ran. Maybe Mrs. Crenshaw would cover the donuts when she was done—if there were any left to cover.

Cecil and Elbert weren't hard to find. Surprisingly, they weren't making much of a mess as they did their chore. Neither one wanted anything to spill on them.

"What do you want?" Cecil sneered.

"Your aunt told me to come and check on you to make sure you're doing a good job." Maggie knew this wasn't exactly true, but she sure didn't want them to know that if they made a mess, she would have to clean it up. If Cecil knew that, he would make a mess on purpose just so she would have to clean it.

"You wait, Maggie Daniels! We'll get even." Cecil pushed past her with the slop bucket. Maggie had to dodge to keep from being hit.

She felt a little sorry for Elbert. Cecil had made him carry the worst bucket. He was sliding his feet along the floor instead of stepping normally, so nothing would splash out.

"What's taking you so long?" Cecil called from the bottom of the stairs.

Elbert had stopped at the top step. He tried first one foot, then the other, but neither seemed to work. "I need you to come help me down the stairs."

"No way! I carried this bucket. That one is yours."

"But I don't know how to do it without spilling it," Elbert wailed.

"That's your problem. I'm gone!" Cecil picked up his bucket and headed out the door. Elbert was pale.

Maggie took a deep breath. "Elbert, I'll hold one side. You hold the other."

Elbert heaved a sigh of relief. "Thanks, Maggie."

When the buckets were emptied, Maggie was glad to take them to the pump outside and wash them out herself. Trying to make Cecil and Elbert do the job would have been more work than it was worth.

"Watch out!"

Maggie stopped swishing the water in the bucket and listened.

"But Aunt Louise told us not to, Cecil."

"You're just scared!"

"I am not!"

Maggie wiped her hands down the sides of her dress and pushed back her hair. "Those boys!" she whispered to the sky. She didn't know what they were doing now, but she knew it was something they shouldn't. She left the buckets and followed the noise.

There was a lot of noise to follow. Cecil and Elbert were halfway up the ten-foot chicken-wire fence that surrounded the turkeys.

"Cecil! Elbert! Get down right now!"

"Try and make us," Cecil challenged.

Maggie stood with her hands on her hips. "Don't budge another inch!"

Cecil climbed higher. The flimsy chicken-wire fence swayed and plunged to the ground. Chaos followed as terrified turkeys swarmed, squawked, scattered, fluttered and ran. Mr. Tom ruffled his feathers, swooped onto Cecil's back and began to drum on Cecil's head with his beak.

"He's killing me! He's killing me!" Cecil darted in circles, trying to rid himself of the turkey. The turkey dug its claws into

Cecil's back in a life-or-death grip and pecked some more.

Elbert scrambled through the wild turkeys and ran to hide behind Maggie, tears of horror in his eyes.

"I suppose you think this is funny, young lady!"

Maggie swung around to face Mrs. Crenshaw.

Mrs. Crenshaw was seething. "My turkeys are everywhere! And look at poor Cecil. You just get yourself over there and get that turkey off of the poor child."

Maggie took a step back.

"Go on. Get that turkey off Cecil!"

"But I didn't put the turkey on him." Maggie didn't know if she was more afraid of the turkey, or Mrs. Crenshaw.

"It was your fault. You were supposed to be watching them."

Maggie's blood pounded in her ears. Slowly, she turned toward the flying Cecil and the flapping turkey. Her eyes fell on a stick. She picked it up, took aim and swung.

"Eeeow!"

She missed the turkey. Cecil grabbed his leg, dropped to the ground and rolled. The turkey lost its grip and sprawled, skidding across the dust on his tail feathers. Maggie sagged with relief. The dust settled.

"Why did you do that?" Cecil demanded as he crawled to his knees.

"Your Aunt Louise told me to save you from the turkey. I did." Maggie turned and walked away.

"But you hit me!" Cecil yelled.

Maggie didn't even look back. "I missed the turkey, but you are safe."

Turkeys scattered across the yard. Maggie didn't care. She wanted this day to be over so she could get paid and go home.

Mrs. Crenshaw stood in front of her with her arms crossed. Her foot tapped, and her eyes shot sparks. "Just what were you thinking, young lady?"

"Ma'am, I was trying to keep the boys out of the turkey pen, but they wouldn't listen to me. They climbed the fence. I told them to get down."

"Cecil, is this true?" Mrs. Crenshaw asked.

Cecil licked his lips.

Maggie knew he was afraid to tell her. "Cecil, you'd better tell her the truth." She mouthed the words so Mrs. Crenshaw wouldn't hear.

"Maggie bet us we couldn't get a feather from that old tom turkey," Cecil lied.

"Margaret Pearl!" Mrs. Crenshaw snatched Maggie's arm.

"I did not!"

"This will be the end of your job. And you can forget your pay. That money will have to go for all the turkeys I've lost today, and to pay someone to gather the ones I have left."

Elbert inched over to stand by Maggie. "She didn't do it."

"What?" Mrs. Crenshaw swiveled her head to stare at Elbert.

He slipped his hand into Maggie's. "Cecil is lying. He wanted to catch a turkey and throw it on Maggie for making us empty the slop buckets."

"You rat!" Cecil shouted.

"Cecil?"

"It was wrong for Maggie to do that to us."

"That is enough, Cecil! I would have been mad at Maggie for that, too, but you aren't going to get back at her by doing something that will hurt someone else. You will talk to your uncle when he gets home, which won't be long from now."

Cecil glared at Maggie, held up his fist and smashed it into his hand.

Mrs. Crenshaw turned to face Maggie. "One more chance! You've got one more chance to prove yourself." She touched her bottom lip. "Maggie, I need some potatoes to fix for dinner. Go get some from the cellar."

Maggie was glad to leave. She didn't want to be around Mrs. Crenshaw or Cecil. Elbert was turning out to be okay. If he hadn't stood up for her, she would be on her way home now with no job and no pay. "Thank you, Elbert," she whispered.

The cellar door was made from old gray boards. It took all Maggie's strength to lift the door and heave it open. Dust splashed when it slammed open against the earth floor. Maggie waited and watched the dust settle. She hesitated. A musty smell rose to meet her as she gazed down into the dark. The cellar was creepy. She swallowed and hoped it would only take a couple of minutes to dash down there, grab the potatoes and run back up.

She stepped down onto the first step. It was made of dirt. The steps had been cut from the earth. She couldn't run on them. She would have to be careful.

Maggie counted the steep steps as her foot touched each one. "Thirteen," she groaned. "Thirteen is not unlucky. Some people just say it is," she whispered, trying to convince herself. She took a deep breath. The air was thick and dank. The only light was the light that filtered down the steps. The cellar was cool, but the cold she felt wasn't from the air temperature. She squinted in search of the potatoes. There they were, in a heap in the middle of the dirt floor. She eased over to the pile, knelt down and started to fill the pockets of her new dress.

Crash!

The cellar door slammed. Dust rolled down the stairs, smothering Maggie.

"Hey!" she choked through her coughs. Her heart stalled, only to resume its pounding, shaking her whole body. She scrambled to the stairs, stumbled up them in the dark and pounded on the cellar door.

"Cecil! Elbert! Open this door right now!" she yelled. Nothing. "Open this door!" Silence.

Maggie tried to push the door up. It would not budge. She pounded with her fists until dust showered over her. "Cecil! Elbert!" Still there was no sound but the pounding of her heart.

The dust settled. Her pulse didn't.

Maybe she could find a stick or shovel, or something to pry the door open. She turned back to the musty cellar, which was now completely dark. She hated the idea of going back down those steps. One more time she shouted into the silence, "Cecil! Elbert! This is not funny anymore!"

Silence rang in her ears.

She stretched her hands to the walls along the sides of the cellar stairs so she could feel her way down. Her hands sank into silky, sticky cobwebs. Wildly, she shook them off. Something crawled up her arm. She screamed and stumbled. Plunging to the bottom of the steps, Maggie smashed against the solid earthen floor and sank into darkness.

CHAPTER 17

Settled Dust

S omething ran across Maggie's face. She wiped it away and forced her eyes open. Darkness. She shuddered and rolled into a tight ball, remembering where she was. Cecil had gotten back at her, all right. How long had she been in this horrible place? Had Mrs. Crenshaw looked for her? What about the potatoes she needed? Maggie shivered. She wasn't really cold—at least, not on the outside. She was cold on the inside. What if no one ever came to find her?

Maggie wrapped her arms around herself. She was shaking like a cottonwood leaf in the Kansas wind. Then she remembered the cobwebs she had stuck her hand through, and suddenly she felt as though spiders were crawling all over her.

Maggie jumped up and stamped. She shouted into the thick silence. Her scream thudded against the sod walls and dwindled into nothing. She stumbled to the pile of potatoes and climbed to the top. Surely bugs and spiders wouldn't bother her up there. For a long time, she stood on top of the pile of potatoes and shouted. Finally, she sank down and cried.

When there were no more tears, she whispered, "Dear God in heaven, I am so scared! I think I hate Cecil. I think I want to ask you to lock him in this cold, dingy cellar after you let me out of here. Please, please let me out of here!" After a pause, she added, "I'm sorry about hating Cecil, and I'm really scared that you'll leave me in this dungeon until I quit hating him. That might take forever." She shivered. "I'll try, but I can't even heap Valina's coals of kindness on him if I'm stuck down here."

She was afraid it sounded as if she were bargaining with God. She shook her head and whispered, "I'm sorry. I'm so sorry!" She dropped her head into her arms. Talking to the God in heaven had helped the God in her heart to calm her. Maggie didn't understand how talking to God could calm her, but it did.

She took a deep breath and looked around. Her eyes had adjusted to the darkness, and shadowy shapes began to form. Quickly, she shut her eyes. She didn't want the shadows to bring the icy fear creeping back again. She didn't know when she fell asleep, but sleep was the warmest, safest place the cold cellar had to offer. On top of the potatoes, she plunged into dream.

A crash of thunder exploded, shattering her dreams. Maggie's eyes flew open as a dust storm rolled down the steps.

"Maggie? Maggie? Maggie?" The sound of her name soaked into the cellar walls like water poured onto drought-thirsty ground. At the top of the chopped dirt steps, someone held a lantern. Sue stumbled down to the cellar.

Maggie flew into Sue's arms. With a flood of tears, she whispered over and over, "Mama! Mama!"

"Margaret Pearl," Sue crooned as she wrapped her arms around Maggie, and nuzzled her hair. "She's here!" Sue called over her shoulder.

Sue stroked Maggie's hair. "We've been looking for you everywhere. When you didn't show up for supper, we searched the pasture. Your daddy and Martin are looking in on the Gatlin place now. We've got to let them know that we found you." She brushed Maggie's hair from her dusty, tear-streaked cheeks. "Maggie, are you all right?"

Maggie had quit shaking. She nodded. "I think so."

"What happened?"

Maggie looked around. The cellar swam with people. Her eyes found Cecil and Elbert. "Mrs. Crenshaw sent me to get potatoes, and I think Cecil and Elbert slammed the cellar door shut. I think they were playing a joke on me."

Every pair of eyes settled on Cecil and Elbert. Cecil kicked at the dirt. Elbert edged behind Cecil.

"Boys?" Mr. Crenshaw's voice boomed. He stepped forward, casting his shadow over them.

Elbert's eyes grew, as if he could see death marching toward him. In fear, he burst out, "Aunt Louise told us to shut the cellar door!"

Heavy silence shrouded the cellar. Maggie's heart beat loudly. Mrs. Crenshaw? Cecil and Elbert, she could understand, but Mrs. Crenshaw was a grown-up. Grown-ups didn't do things like that.

"What?" Mr. Crenshaw loomed over Elbert.

"Aunt Louise told us to shut the cellar door. She said that if we did, she would let us have the donuts."

"What?" All eyes searched for Mrs. Crenshaw. She had backed against the dirt wall.

"Aunt Louise told us she'd let Maggie out after a bit and send her home," Cecil added.

"We thought that she was long gone," Elbert chimed in.

"Honest!" Cecil swore.

Mr. Crenshaw took a step toward his wife. "Louise?"

Mrs. Crenshaw's breath caught. "I ... I just wanted to teach her a lesson."

"Lord have mercy on your soul!" Valina's rich voice sounded the thoughts of everyone in the cellar.

"Just what kind of lesson did you want to teach her, Louise?" Mr. Crenshaw spread his hands wide.

"Oh, I don't know. She just always bounces into my house every day so ... so..."

"So happy? So kind? So cheerful?" Mr. Crenshaw finished for her. "Louise, you could learn a few lessons from Maggie. She has brought a delight into our home that we have never had."

"But she's just a little girl. How could she do that?" Mrs. Crenshaw whined.

"I'm eleven," Maggie whispered. She pulled away from Sue and went to stand in front of Mrs. Crenshaw.

"Louise, you could ask her." Mr. Crenshaw spoke quietly.

Mrs. Crenshaw looked at Maggie. A single tear edged over the woman's blotchy cheek.

"Go ahead, Louise. Ask her how she has managed to stay so happy every day, when you have treated her the way you have." Mr. Crenshaw was firm.

"What ..." Mrs. Crenshaw stumbled and began again. "What could you teach me?"

"I could teach you how to have the God up in heaven become the God in your heart. My mama taught me." Maggie glanced at Sue.

Sue held her head high, wiped her face and stepped to stand

beside her daughter. She took Maggie's hand.

"Lord Almighty! That girl done got herself a mama." Valina's voice sang through the dark cellar.

Maggie felt the moist tears on Sue's hands. They brought warmth and courage to her heart. She stretched her hand to Mrs. Crenshaw. "Do you want to learn?"

Time stood waiting.

"Louise?" Mr. Crenshaw whispered.

Mrs. Crenshaw's quivering hand snatched at her throat. "You are a mere child. I know more about God than you will ever hope to know. I've been going to church all my life. You have no right to claim that you can teach me things about God." Mrs. Crenshaw pushed Maggie's hand aside and shoved past her. She ran up the dirt steps and disappeared.

Mr. Crenshaw shook his head while he gazed at the empty steps. "I had hoped…" He turned to Maggie. "I'm very sorry, Maggie. I don't understand why she did this." He dropped his head and paused before he continued. "Maggie, will you be pressing charges against Louise?"

"Charges? You mean charges that would send her to jail?"

Mr. Crenshaw nodded.

Valina nodded. "Hmph! That would sure teach her a lesson. Put that fine, upstanding woman behind bars."

Maggie shook her head. "Mr. Crenshaw, that would hurt you. And what would you do with Cecil and Elbert? If Cecil and Elbert left, I wouldn't have a job. I need my job."

"Do you mean that you would consider still working for Louise?" Mr. Crenshaw asked with awe.

Valina gasped.

Sue stepped in. "Her daddy might have something to say

about that."

Maggie turned to Sue. "I need the job to keep my daddy here."

Sue shook her head. "Maggie, I don't know if your daddy will let you work for Mrs. Crenshaw after what has happened tonight."

"Does he have to know?" Maggie pleaded.

"We do not keep secrets from each other," Sue said quietly.

Maggie persisted. "What if Mr. Crenshaw were my boss, instead of Mrs. Crenshaw?"

Sue looked at Mr. Crenshaw. Maggie begged him with her eyes.

"Well, I'll be!" Mr. Crenshaw smiled. "Do you know what a treasure you have here?"

Sue slid her arm around Maggie. "My little girl is a treasure I value very much. She is a gem. A pearl!"

"Well, Miss Daniels." Mr. Crenshaw knelt on one knee in front of her. "We will have to make this an offer that will be hard for your daddy to refuse. What would you say if I doubled your pay?"

Maggie gasped.

He continued, "If I am right, that would make it two dollars a day?"

"Yes, sir!"

"Two dollars?" Cecil whistled.

"It should be more, Cecil, for all she has to put up with from you. Just how many times has she saved your hide?"

Cecil shrugged his shoulders and dropped his gaze to the floor.

Mr. Crenshaw chuckled and went on, "Maggie, I am assuming that Louise has not paid you yet."

Maggie shook her head.

Mr. Crenshaw dug in his pocket and whisked out his wallet. He took a twenty-dollar bill and handed it to Maggie. "Will this cover what Louise owes you?"

"That is way more than Mrs. Crenshaw owes me." Maggie pushed the twenty back toward Mr. Crenshaw.

"After what you've been through, it is well earned." Mr. Crenshaw folded her fingers over the bill and patted her hand, as if to seal the bargain.

"Mama?" Maggie looked at Sue. Sue nodded.

Maggie had never held so much money in her whole life. Quickly, she shoved it deep into the pocket of her overall dress and snapped it shut.

"Mr. Crenshaw, Maggie has told me that you are a nice man. Thank you for what you have done for her." Sue stretched out her hand to shake Mr. Crenshaw's.

"Mrs. Daniels, Maggie has brought joy into our home. Thank you for sharing her with us." Mr. Crenshaw turned to Maggie. "I'll see you Monday morning, if your father agrees."

"Yes, sir!" Maggie giggled.

"Well, I for one have had enough of this cellar. Ladies, I'll go get the sedan and drive you home." Mr. Crenshaw motioned for the ladies to head up the stairs.

Cecil zoomed past them. Mr. Crenshaw snatched his ear. "Eeow!"

"Ladies first, my boy!"

Sue reached for Maggie's hand. "Margaret Pearl?"

"Mama," Maggie beamed. She couldn't help looking at Valina. Valina had told her that the time would come when it would feel right to call Sue Mama. Now it felt right. It made her feel warm,

as though fireworks were exploding her heart.

Valina winked. "God is a God of miracles."

At the top of the earthen steps, Maggie took a deep breath, swirled around and gazed at the star-speckled sky.

"Maggie?"

She felt a tug on her dress. Elbert stood at her side.

"Elbert?"

"Maggie, you've been nice all the time, even when we weren't nice to you. We did terrible things to you, and you just kept bringing us treats, like pies and jelly and donuts. Maggie, I'm sorry for all the bad things I did to you. I promise I won't do them anymore."

"Elbert, that's okay, but you really ought to be telling this to God. Those bad things are sin. He's the one who can forgive you for that, not me."

"If I tell God I'm sorry, can you teach me how to have God in my heart?" he whispered.

Maggie smiled. "Elbert, if you tell Him you're sorry for all those sins and ask Him to come into your heart, He will be in your heart. Then I won't have to teach you. He will!"

"Maggie, how do I talk to God?"

Maggie shrugged. "You just talk to Him like you do to me."

"But I can't see Him, Maggie."

Maggie spread her arms wide. "Elbert, God is all around. He's in heaven. He's here. He's everywhere!"

Elbert threw his head back and shouted to the stars, "Dear God that is everywhere, I'm sorry for everything I ever did to Maggie and Cecil and Mom and … and everybody. Would you please come be in my heart?"

After a silence, Elbert pulled his face from the night sky

and beamed at Maggie with joy and relief. Maggie grabbed his hands, and together they swung in circles until they fell in a heap.

Maggie looked up. Valina stood over her. "Mrs. Valina, they worked! The heaping coals—they worked!"

Valina's rich laughter rang out. "Lord God Almighty! He done promised they'd work in His own time. Them heaping coals, them heaping coals! The Lord sure put power in them heaping coals!"

"Valina, what are you talking about?" Sue asked.

Valina's eyes sought Maggie. Quickly, Maggie put a finger to her lips to remind Valina of her promise not to tell. The rumble of Mr. Crenshaw's black sedan came to the rescue.

Valina swallowed. "Mrs. Sue, here comes Mr. Crenshaw in that contraption of his, so I don't have time to explain right now. You come over for tea sometime, and I'll be telling you." Valina turned to head down the lane while the getting was good. Sue's mouth dropped open at how smartly Valina had put her off.

Maggie tore down the lane to catch Valina. "It worked, Valina! The heaping coals—they worked! But what about Cecil and Mrs. Crenshaw? What about them?"

"We have to wait for His time. Some folks need more coals poured on them than others. We'll keep on heaping those coals, and it's bound to work, just like the good Lord done told us. Now you better get back to that mama of yours. She's full of questions." Valina winked.

"I love you, Valina!" Maggie turned and ran.

"I love you, too, child, like you was my very own," Valina whispered.

Maggie followed Sue into Mr. Crenshaw's sedan. Elbert scrambled in to join them. Sitting in the auto, Maggie leaned back. "Wow," she thought, "another first!" She had never ridden in a car before. She had never felt right about calling Sue Mama before. She had never had a friend like Valina before. She had never held a twenty-dollar bill before, and she had never taught someone how to have God in his heart before.

Kerwhap! The black sedan hit a rut. Maggie crashed into Elbert and giggled. "Wow!" she shouted—to Elbert, to Mama, to Mr. Crenshaw and to anyone else who might hear her. "I love payday!"

Don't miss the exciting sequel to
In the Shadow of the Enemy

*M*aggie stayed in the shadows and made her way to the side of the shed. She pressed herself against the wall and edged around to the back. She peeked around the corner and saw a man with a shovel digging against the rugged foundation, and then sighed with relief. It was Daddy! That must be why their milk cow, Lulubelle, hadn't been bothered by the noise. She stepped out boldly. "Daddy, what are you doing?"

As the man twisted around to face her, he yelled, "What do you…" Swiftly he raised the shovel like a spear and flung it at Maggie.

When Secrets Come Home
Book 3 in the Gatlin Fields series
Available now from
www.sablecreekpress.com

Don't miss the exciting sequel to
When Secrets Come Home

*M*aggie thought her lungs would burst, and all she could hear was her own pounding heart. Suddenly she felt the cold steel of the railroad tracks vibrate under her bare feet. The startled girl froze as a train whistle blasted through her heartbeats. The train's light glared as it bolted around the curve, heading straight toward her.

"Run, Maggie, run!" Jed shouted. Maggie shook.

After the Dust Settles
Book 4 in the Gatlin Fields series
Available now from
www.sablecreekpress.com

"*God* HAS A PLAN FOR OUR LIVES, A BEAUTIFUL WILL FOR HOW WE SHOULD LIVE, BUT FINDING HIS WILL IS NOT SOMETHING THAT JUST HAPPENS. WE CAN DETERMINE WE ARE GOING TO BE OBEDIENT. AS *His Word* TAKES ROOT INWARDLY, WE CAN LIVE IT OUTWARDLY."

CHALLENGING THOUGHTS FOR TEEN GIRLS

THINK ON THESE *Things*

JAN VAN HEE

CPSIA information can be obtained at www.ICGtesting.com
Printed in the USA
LVOW041736230412

278790LV00011B/166/P